HOUSE OF MADNESS

House of Madness
Copyright © 2019
Sara Harris

Library of Congress Control Number: 2019930527

Cover concept and design by David Warren.

Published by WordCrafts Press
Cody, Wyoming 82414
www.wordcrafts.net

House
of
MADNESS

A GHOST STORY

Sara Harris

WordCrafts

*There are more things in heaven and earth, Horatio, than are
dreampt of in your philosophy.*

Hamlet
Act 1, Scene 5

CHAPTER ONE

THE BEGINNING

W*ould you just unlock these back doors already?*

The words were dangerously close to finding their way off Adelaide's tongue as she sat in the back of the realtor's blacker-than-night Cadillac. She spun her wedding ring, the princess cut half-carat, around her finger as the Realtor, Kim something, rattled on in her nasal voice. The more Kim talked, the quicker her voice climbed Adelaide's top-ten list of things she disliked. Currently, it ranked somewhere between monthly cramps and waiting in line at the DMV.

Adelaide shifted her attention out the tinted back window to the front yard of the house she knew they couldn't afford. But Tim wanted to see it, so here they were. The springtime wind swayed the boughs of the old shade trees, elm if she remembered her leaves correctly. Their shadows danced over the steep concrete driveway, pushed first one way then pulled back the other. Her husband's voice from the front seat interrupted her trance-like reverie.

"You said it was built when? Did you hear that honey?"

"Um, no." Adelaide forced a smile. "I must have missed it."

Tim spoke to Kim. "My wife's an author. She loves history. Tell her what you told me. About the house."

Adelaide shook her head. *To be called an author would imply I had something published.* She tried not to look at Kim's arched eyebrows, bespeaking her feigned interest. *Right now I'm more like an unemployed school teacher who will need to start handing out resumes if someone doesn't pick up my work soon.*

The faces of Adelaide's students back in Dallas popped into her mind without warning. Sure, they tried to poison her coworker, but she still missed them. *If I had her as my teacher, I may have tried to do the same.* That teacher was a screamer, always degrading. Always telling them how stupid they were. Those kids may have been from the wrong side of the tracks, but they were far but dumb and knew when they were being insulted.

"Wonderful," Kim chirped. "I bet you write bodice rippers, don't you Abby."

Adelaide nodded as the faces of her former students fizzled from her mind. *Addie. Not Abby.*

"Not quite. ***A Heart on Hold*** is a historical romance set during the Civil War. The hero, Sanderson, goes off to war and leaves his love, our heroine Charlotte, behind. When he is taken captive by an unexpected Yankee and Charlotte receives word that he died at Alton Prison in Illinois, she refuses to accept it. With just her horse and her faith, she leaves Arkansas behind and heads north through an unwelcoming world to find her love and bring him home—one way or another."

Kim stared at her in the rearview. "My, that's a farfetched little love story, isn't it?"

"Actually, Sanderson's life follows that of real Confederate Captain E.A. Adams—"

"You know," Kim interrupted, "I have been meaning to write a book myself."

Any time somebody learned she was an aspiring author, she was suddenly privy to all of their own unrealized writing dreams. *A Heart on Hold is going to be a four-book series, too. Every one of them would probably be over your head anyway.*

"It would be entitled, *Adventures in an Empty House*. In it, I would tell all about the people I've met and adventures I've had since becoming a Realtor." Kim winked at her. "But I better not tell you any more, you might steal my ideas."

Not entitled. Titled. To be entitled would mean the book was owed something.

Kim clapped her perfectly manicured hands. The baby-pink color that dotted her nails was the same shade of lipstick that dotted her teeth. "Oh my, we've gotten off topic, haven't we?" She adjusted her hefty frame in the seat. "I was telling your delightful husband that this house was one of the first ranch-style homes in the city. Before Big Spring was a city, really. It was constructed in 1889."

Adelaide straightened her back. One of her favorite topics to teach was Texas History. Especially the European migration. Most of the Germans settled further east, in the true Hill Country. A handful had continued west despite the heavy Indian presence and general lawlessness that plagued the land. The French came through in droves, leaving their undeniable mark, but most continued on to already established bigger cities. Austrians, Romanians, and a handful of Italian families also made the journey across Texas at the end of the nineteenth century.

Kim, however, didn't pause in her spiel. "Then, this house was renovated to its current glory in the 1940's by Doctors Roland and Marjorie Darkland. They were such wonderful people. They are the ones responsible for what the house has become today."

Finally, she paused for a breath.

Tim raised a finger. "What about the mental institution we passed on the way in? It seems pretty close. We moved from Dallas for the small-town atmosphere and need a safe house." He glanced back at his wife and daughter.

A house without all the memories. Somewhere to start fresh.

The Realtor chimed to life. "Oh, that old insane asylum? It's been set for demolition."

From the backseat, Adelaide stared at Kim's hair. *How does it manage to stay in that fancy updo in this wind?* Kim's floral perfume filled the car and was beginning to weigh on Adelaide like an iron jacket. Tim and Addie's daughter, Michaela, cupped her eleven-year-old hands around her mouth and slumped in the backseat. Smells always bothered her.

I never figured how women could put on a cloud of perfume. Do they spray it on with a fogger? Being female herself, Addie figured she must have missed that day of school since she had never learned that particular technique. She offered Michaela an apologetic smile.

Kim waved her hands as though she was waving away a problematic fly. Every time she moved, the perfume smell intensified. "They transferred the last patient to Crestview *months* ago."

A rash of goosebumps cropped up on Adelaide's skin. She'd come across the name Crestview Home when she was researching Big Spring, Texas prior to their move. Crestview was the hospital in the Spring Town Gazette not long ago and the press coverage hadn't been positive. The story told of a patient who starved to death, restrained to his bed by his wrists and ankles. The police were investigating the hospital for neglect and at least one suit had already been filed for wrongful death.

Michaela held her breath until her cheeks puffed out like

a chipmunk's and patted her mother's hand. She pointed out the window. A pair of gray squirrels chased each other from a leafy elm tree across the lush grass and up an obscured black line that led from the ground, up the bricks, and disappeared into the attic.

That's a strange place for a wire.

Addie and Michaela shared a look. "That looks like a great tree for a fort," Addie whispered.

Michaela exhaled the breath she'd been holding. "Yes, it does," she whispered back.

Kim was still droning on in the front seat about the mental hospital and paid their whispers no mind. "You know, the couple that refurbished this house, the Darkland doctors I mentioned earlier, worked there. At the old mental institution. They were so brilliant."

Tim cocked his head. "Brilliant?"

"Oh yes. They ruled over those crazies and kept the place in check. They also came up with new drug therapies to treat those ..." She wrinkled her nose. "Those *patients*."

"They must have been *some* people."

"Oh, we went to church together for *years*. Always on the front row, they were. Until they retired to Jamaica. It's their kids—the two boys are doctors of course, but their daughter is a lawyer—they are the ones who are selling this place."

Ah, that's why it's in our price range.

Kim looked almost reverent for a moment. "Must be nice, huh? I suppose all of us are in the wrong line of work. Shall we go in?" Kim pressed the unlock button and Michaela flung her door open and let the fresh air rush in.

"Wow, we are actually looking at owning a doctor's house!" Tim's voice was edged in a contagious brand of excitement. "Did you ever think we'd be able to do this?"

Addie stepped over the row of newly sprouted tulips that lined the flower bed and answered honestly. "No. And I'm not sure we can now."

Kim fiddled with the lockbox as Michaela watched intently. Tim turned his wife around, his hand around her waist. "Just look at this front yard."

From nowhere, a chorus of birds sang to life. They swooped and dove from one magnificent tree to the next, some carrying nesting material, others just singing. The flowerbeds were meticulously maintained and boasted sweet-scented honeysuckle that twined around a deep green woody hedge that was sprinkled with bright red berries. Shady and built on a gentle slope, or perhaps just landscaped that way, the front yard stretched for almost the entire block in either direction and had all the curb appeal of a quaint park.

Addie's husband gave her a squeeze. "I can't believe it's in our price range."

"I thought it was a little *over* our budget?"

Kim bested the lockbox and the little silver key clattered to the porch.

Michaela bent to retrieve it. "Wow, this is an old key." Sure enough, she held an old fashioned skeleton key in her hand.

Kim snatched it from her palm. "There now. Ready folks?"

Michaela shot inside, but immediately ground to a halt. Her fingers pinched her nose. "Ew, that stinks."

Addie stepped into open, muted yellow kitchen. "Goodness, that's a strong smell. Are we sure nobody else is here?"

Tim joined her. "That's a man's cologne all right. But it's

more like something my grandfather would have worn." He looked at Kim for an explanation.

Kim stepped inside and shrugged her shoulders. Her Pepto-Bismol pink suit jacket strained against any movement. "This place has been vacant for months." She glanced at the outdated yellow countertop that looked to be a mile long. "No other Realtors have left their cards, so it doesn't appear to be recently shown." She wore a look of genuine surprise. "I honestly don't know what that smell is."

Michaela unpinched her nose and turned to her left. "Hey look, a huge bathroom!"

Tim and Kim trailed after the sprightly youngster, but something about the kitchen was too captivating for Adelaide not to admire. The galley kitchen featured a fifteen-foot bar with wooden pull-downs that were stuck in varying positions.

Those are called pass-throughs, I believe. Very old-time.

The double sink was opposite the bar, so a mother could do the breakfast dishes as soon as her family ate. Provided they sat at the bar. Adelaide smiled and let her fingers dance along the wooden cabinets above the long bar.

So much storage.

Behind her, rows of windows lined the wall and allowed a peek into the park-like yard from over the stove and counters. A double oven, also yellow, stared out from the far wall nearest the tiny pantry. Addie opened the tall, thin doors. A series of short shelves sat before her. *Not much pantry.* A shadow beside the shelving caught her eye. She looked closer. *Wait a second.* Addie reached in and gave a tug. The pantry swung toward her, revealing two more rows of shelves and a tiny room.

A movable wall!

Her mouth fell open. Before she could call out to Tim, Michaela's voice echoed off the custom tile floor. "Mom. This bathroom —it *has* to be mine." The eleven-year-old flash of girl appeared at her side. Addie joined in with Michaela's enthusiasm. "There's a stained-glass window, a see-through shower and up-and-down lights that look like they're right out of the fifties!"

Excitement rounded her eyes to the size of tea saucers. "And come look over here. Miss Kim said it could be a play-room or homework room."

Addie pushed the pantry doors shut and turned to follow Michaela. An icy puff brushed her face as she followed her skipping daughter down the length of the bar.

At least the air conditioner works.

An odd sensation brought her to a pause. Michaela rushed on ahead, half skipping and half running. Ever slow, Addie turned and glanced over her shoulder into the empty kitchen. The feeling of someone, just out of sight and sharing space with her, was strong.

Is somebody watching me?

Another chill made her hug her chest. Something *thunked*. "Come on, Mom!"

Addie turned her back to the kitchen and rushed to catch up with Michaela. She pushed the niggle of uneasiness to the back of her mind.

Surely that was just one of the shelves in the pantry falling back into place.

Tim and Kim stepped out of the bathroom, deep in conversation about clay pipes, clogged drains, and how much it would *actually* cost to replace that lead-lined custom stained-glass window, should something horrific befall it.

"Look!" Michaela pushed a corner of the plain-looking wood. It swung outward and revealed a pull-down desk, complete with a lamp and pencil sharpener. "They all do it!" She rushed down the line, pressing the wood and letting the doors swing free. "Cabinets everywhere!"

Addie smiled, but didn't relax her arms. "I see where you'll be doing your homework every day."

Michaela nodded, her blonde wisps of hair brushing across her forehead in rhythm. "And look at the view."

The entire back side of the playroom, as Michaela called it, was lined with windows. And they didn't stop there. Addie trailed behind Tim and Kim as they meandered through the open-concept home into the formal dining room. The floor-to-ceiling windows continued into this room and made up the entire back wall.

"Notice the paint in this room." Kim stroked her chubby fingers along the walls. "It looks golden, doesn't it? Watch when the sunlight hits it."

As if on cue, the clouds shifted in the sky and the room filled with sunshine. Rays bounced off the walls, illuminating the painted-over panels with thousands of tiny sparkles. Tim, Addie, and Michaela gasped in concert.

"I've never seen paint like that," Addie breathed. It seemed to her that the sparkles were tiny nuggets of gold just hidden in the wood.

Perhaps Tim was right to insist on coming to this house, after all. "Golden sparkly paint."

"Very retro," Kim agreed. "If you'll look through here, this is the living space."

"Wait." Addie pointed to a door in the corner of the dining room. "What's this?"

Kim pranced over, her high heels clicking on the flagstone tile. "This, Adelaide, is storage." She turned the knob and opened the wooden door.

Addie peered in, Michaela at her elbow. The girl spoke first. "Carpeted storage? I have never seen a closet like this. It could be a room by itself."

And she was right. Addie and Michaela stepped in. "Look, there's a safe." Michaela fell to her knees to examine its entrails. Addie continued, turning like a ballerina in a music box in the dim space. "And look here, these doors lock—from the inside."

The annoyed creases smoothed from Kim's forehead and she stepped inside. "Really?"

Tim followed. "Those are automatic locks. See?"

He pulled the door shut behind him. At once, they were cloaked in complete darkness.

"Hey," Michaela grumbled. "I almost had it, Dad."

In the confines of the room, someone's breathing was coming faster and faster. Addie put her hand out to steady herself. It bumped something metal on the wall.

A chain clinked somewhere in the dark, followed by Tim's voice. "And then He said, *Let there be light.*" The door swung open and muted slants of sunlight flowed into the dank little room. "How odd is that."

Kim clinked back into the dining room and flipped through her sheaf of papers. "I believe this is a safe room," she muttered. "I don't remember reading about it, though."

Unfazed by the dark, Michaela still fiddled with the safe in the corner.

"Tim, look," Addie whispered. She ran her fingers along the metal box she'd accidentally discovered. "It says Emergency

Call Box." Her eyes widened. "Could this be a secret phone line?"

Tim opened his mouth, but Kim interrupted them. "Well, now that's an adventure, isn't it? Let's see the rest of the house, shall we?"

Michaela rose, defeated. "There's nothing in the safe," she proclaimed. Her voice was thick with more than a little disappointment. Addie patted her daughter.

Kim led them back through the formal dining room and through the giant opening that couldn't be called a doorway in the normal sense of the word. They emerged in the over-sized and equally bright living room. Kim pointed out the unique lighting system which was designed to illuminate by shining up at the ceiling then reflecting down from what Addie thought was just fancy shelving near the ceiling.

"I've never seen lights like that, either. Normal lights shine down. These shine from the top." With each little hidden gem, she was having a harder and harder time concealing her excitement. Addie scarcely noticed the hand-laid rock fireplace that commanded the attention of the room. "What's next?"

"Right this way and I'll show you the master bedroom. There is another bathroom on your right."

Another breath of cold air brushed Adelaide's face as they walked down a tiny hallway that circled around the outside of the dining room. Sure enough, there was another giant bathroom complete with separate vanity and a mirror that took up the entire wall. Another lead-lined stained-glass window stared at them from the far wall. "It certainly is cool in here."

Kim stepped from the flagstone tile onto the thick carpet of the master bedroom, not giving anyone much time to explore the bathroom. More windows lined one wall, while half windows graced the other two exposed walls. A pair of deep walk-in closets took up the fourth. "They built the house with cement walls, so it holds the chill."

Addie glanced at the windows. From here, you could see into the dining room and over into the playroom and kitchen. It was strangely eerie and comforting at the same time. The deep window ledges were wide enough to hold a real flower pot and the rivets had been painted over.

Wait, rivets?

"Steel reinforced windows?"

"Looks like it," Tim agreed.

From their windows, they could see the lone mountain in Big Spring towering above the horizon, looming over them like a child about to vomit. If they walked out of their back yard and across the street, they would be standing at its base. Addie and Tim stared, mesmerized.

"Maybe they needed to keep the storms out," Tim ventured. "I'm sure the winds come whipping down that mountain. Or something."

Or something.

Michaela's voice trilled from another room and echoed off the cement walls. "Look, is this a dressing area?"

Addie hurried through the doorway that beckoned from the back of the master. Shoulder high closets gave the dressing area the feel of a locker room. A tiny sink stood in the corner with mirrors above it. Addie looked in the mirror and saw out the recessed picture window behind her that she hadn't known was there. A family of cardinals were flitting about a nest in an Indian Hawthorne bush just outside. A smile crept over her lips.

Magic around every corner.

Kim strode in. "She's right. This was the lady doctor's dressing area. Continue on through and you'll find the bath."

"Kind of hidden, isn't it?" Addie tried the pocket door. It was painted shut. "Guess it's a good thing since this door doesn't close."

Michaela pushed between them and began opening door after door in the pink and blue bathroom. A curtainless tub sat naked and exposed in an alcove and a half-wall separated the bathing area from the toilet. On that half-wall was more floor to ceiling storage. "Check out this pull-out hamper—it's huge!" A gush of air whooshed out and Michaela coughed. "Musty though."

She let the hamper fall shut with a bang. "Smells like someone put their dirty socks in there and left them for half a year."

Kim turned away from Michaela and shrugged. "She must have liked her privacy." Before she could usher everyone out of the odd and secluded bathroom, Kim did a double take at the light that lit the room. "That's funny. I could have sworn they said the electricity was cut from this place." She flicked the switch. The light went off. An uneasy dimness fell around them.

Addie reached for the switch but hesitated. Her fingers fell lightly on it before flipping it up. Nothing happened.

"That's funny." Kim tried it a couple more times. "Must have been a fluke."

A cold shiver danced down Addie's spine. "You said before that it's been vacant awhile. Is that a *long* while?"

Michaela led the way out of the bathroom. "Now I want to see my room."

Kim followed, oblivious to Michaela's excitable demand. "Yes, it's been empty several months now. Almost six."

"So, it probably wasn't the air conditioner I felt earlier?"

She shook her head, her bouffant hair wiggling precariously. "Impossible." She tried the switch again. Still nothing.

If there had been a clock in the house, Addie could have heard the seconds click by.

"Old houses are drafty," Kim began. "And this one is old."

The echo of Tim's voice made them both jump. "Check this out! I found another safe room."

Without speaking, they strode back through the bedroom and into the tiny hall with Michaela dancing along in front of them. "Where are you Dad? I'm lost!"

"Down here, Kiddo."

His voice seemed to come from everywhere and nowhere at the same time.

Had she turned right, Michaela would have gone back into the living room part of the house. She turned left. Addie quickened her pace to catch up.

"All right Dad, I'm com—" Michaela started. Her words died in her throat. She ground to a halt in the middle of what looked like a room but was far too open. More like a hidden den with two giant closets and a cable connection. Addie almost ran into her.

"Wow," she mouthed. "I want this room. I've never—"

"Seen anything like it," mother and daughter finished together.

None of us have seen anything like it. Anything like this house.

Tim appeared from yet another unrealized hallway even farther down. "Keep on coming, the house isn't done with us yet."

Michaela led the way, unwilling or unable to turn her face from the quaint little room. The entire hallway had been whitewashed at some point, including the doorknobs. A few steps into the deepening darkness, Tim knocked on a door. If someone was running through the house in a blind dash, they would probably miss this doorway all together.

"Check this out." Tim turned the knob and flicked on his phone's flashlight app. It cast an eerie glow over the room that could pass as a closet—but so clearly wasn't.

Kim pushed past Addie, her mouth agape. She didn't even take the trouble to feign politeness. "What the—"

"Cool! Can I see?" Michaela's chipper voice broke the strange sensation that buzzed within the room. "Hey," she pressed her skinny frame between her father and mother and slid into the room. "What's that?"

All gazes fell to where her finger pointed. A box, white-washed like everything else, protruded off the far wall, like a doll's bench. It was built-in and appeared to be both nailed and painted shut. Michaela turned around and pointed above the double doors, continuing the thought she hadn't bothered to speak, yet everyone had heard just the same; *It locks from the inside in here, too.*"

A sudden sense of claustrophobia choked Addie and she stumbled backward into the dark hall. Gasps caught in her throat but refused to follow through to her lungs. A very real sensation of suffocating widened her eyes.

Kim's voice sounded like a wounded bird. "Is she choking?"

Tim and Michaela's voices were far away and melded into one harmonizing sound. "Mom ... Honey ..."

The edges of Addie's vision started to dim. Still, she gasped like a fish out of water.

"Should we do the Heimlich... She's turning blue..."

Another icy burst of wind, like one that comes from standing in front of a swamp cooler as it comes on, hit her in the face. A welcome swoosh of air swept down her burning throat into her chest. She sucked it in, breathing the sweet relief with tears in her eyes.

Tim, Kim, and Michaela stared down at her. Apparently in her struggle to breathe, Addie slid down the wall and wound up on the chilly tile.

"Mama, are you all right?"

Tim reached to help her up. "Here Adelaide."

Addie took his hand and struggled to her feet. "I'm fine," she rasped. "That was strange. I haven't had a panic attack in a decade. Or maybe more."

Bull. You know when you had your last panic attack Adelaide. That miscarriage did a number on you. What's it been, six months now?

Addie dropped Tim's hand and studied the tilework at their feet. She brushed her hands over her flat stomach, smoothing imaginary wrinkles from her Volleyball Mom shirt, as Michaela scampered off into the back recesses of the house. "Let's keep going."

The back of the house held a deeper cool than the rest of it. Perhaps because of the concrete walls. Perhaps because of the distinct lack of floor-to-ceiling windows.

Or perhaps something else.

Addie shrugged off the thought. *What else could it be? There isn't any logical reason why it would be anything else—so why think about it? Plus, you don't even believe in that hoodoo stuff.*

"Two more bedrooms are back here," Kim announced. "Along with another bathroom, and of course, more storage."

Addie stepped into the first bedroom. Lots of windows, but of a normal size. Michaela stood in the center of the room, a wide smile on her face. The lanky girl turned slow circles as though she'd found herself in a middle of a ballroom instead of just a regular room.

"This is it; this is my room," she breathed.

Tim smiled and crossed his arms. "What about the other room, the one without a wall?"

Michaela shook her head. "This is the one. It's been waiting for me."

Addie closed the space between them. "Come on, let's see the last of the house."

"I'll wait here. I love this room."

Addie and Tim shared a look that clearly said, *It's you she takes after*. Addie shrugged.

Kim checked her watch. "We should have been done fifteen minutes ago. Come along, family. Chop chop."

Addie suppressed an eye roll and followed the clinking woman down the tile hall to the last of the rooms. The second bedroom was a mirror-image of the first, except with two closets instead of one. The bathroom that capped off the hall featured a hidden toilet, sunken shower, and double sinks. True to her word, Michaela didn't bother to see the rest of the house. *Wild horses couldn't pull her out of that room.*

Kim turned to them and huffed. "So, tell me." Annoyance contorted her perfectly made up features into something that resembled a Picasso painting. "Are y'all interested in purchasing this home?"

Tim and Addie stared at one another.

You know you love it, Addie. Tim wiggled his eyebrows.

Addie arched hers. *But it's so expensive—*

He cocked his head in response. *Hidden rooms, sparkly paint, a park for a front yard.* "The little den without a wall would make a perfect writing nook," Tim whispered. He winked.

Kim checked her pink sparkly phone. "Three more messages have come in since we've been here, all requesting to see *this* house."

Adelaide closed her eyes and offered an infinitesimal nod of approval.

Tim squared his shoulders and faced Kim. "Tell them it's off the market. The Smithfield family got it first."

Defeated, Addie's heart thudded faster and faster until it galloped within her chest. Dollar signs, old pipes, and something she couldn't quite place all melded together in her mind, swirling, until—

Tim's voice echoed in the dank hallway. "Sounds good. Kim, if you don't mind dropping us back at our car, we'll meet you back at your office in half an hour to sign the papers."

Kim led them down the hall to a tucked-away door beside Michaela's room. "We can go out this door here. Then I'll lock up."

"Geez, the surprises are never ending," Tim managed. He pulled the heavy purple door open wide. They emerged at the far end of the park-like front yard. Deep greenery surrounded them, almost concealing the door all together.

"Oh, let me get Michaela." Addie stepped back inside and turned into the room Michaela claimed as her own. "Come on baby, let's—"

Michaela was gone.

"Mack?" Addie's pulse threatened to race. "Macky?"

Soft whispers met her ears. The closet door was open just a crack.

Addie flung it open wide. "Macky?"

Michaela sat cross-legged in the corner of the darkened closet. The light glinted off of a mirror that hung on the back side of the door. She squinted up at her mother and shielded her eyes with her hand. "Hey."

"Whatcha doin', Baby Girl?" Addie's voice took on the tone she used when Michaela was an infant. "I couldn't find you."

"Exploring. And stuff."

Addie forced a smile. Normally Michaela wouldn't sit still for anything, especially not in a strange house. To find her holed up in a dark closet gave Addie pause.

"It's time to go, Baby."

"Okay."

Michaela made no move to get up. Addie opened the closet door wider.

"I'll be there in a second, Mom."

Addie ignored the tiny voice in her head that said, *Pick up your daughter, run out of this room,* and widened her pasted-on smile.

"Everyone's outside waiting, don't be long. Okay?"

Michaela simply stared at her, so Addie turned and strode from the room. She didn't go outside, though. She tucked herself just behind the lip of the door, her back pressed to the chilled concrete wall, and listened.

More muttering, muffled and quiet. Scraping. *Thunk,* as the closet door closed, *squeak* as it opened again.

Michaela's sing-song voice was subdued. *"Au revoir mon ami."*

Addie pulled out her phone and opened a translator app. *It's French. Goodbye my friend.*

Tiny hairs on the back of Addie's neck rose like hackles as Michaela emerged.

"That was good French, Macky."

Michaela's eyes narrowed to wary slits. "Were you spying on me?"

"Didn't want you to get turned around in this house, is all." She hesitated. "Where did you learn that?"

Michaela shrugged as though speaking a foreign phrase with a spot-on accent to an empty room was completely normal. "Did we get the house?"

Addie nodded as worried knots formed in her gut. "Y-yes." She smiled, hopefully in a convincing manner. "Dad made sure we got it. We go sign the papers in a bit."

Michaela's thick brown brows furrowed. "Good. I'm glad."

They stepped outside together. Kim was locking all the doors, checking and rechecking this and that, and Tim was already in the black Cadillac.

CHAPTER TWO

Moving In

"You know," Tim's voice was thoughtful as they watched Kim's Cadillac squeal out of the parking lot of their hotel, "we didn't explore the backyard."

Michaela and Addie swiveled their heads to look at him.

He wiggled his eyebrows. "Apparently, our Realtor has some business to attend to before we can sign our paperwork. That gives us just enough time to stop by the drive-in for a coke ..." His voice trailed off and mixed with a hot swirl of West Texas air.

Addie wrung her hands and looked down at Michaela's upturned face. "Whatdaya say, Macky? Want to go explore the backyard before we sign the papers?"

A slow smile spread across her lips and brightened her ice blue eyes. "Let's do it."

One quick stop later and the Smithfield-Mobile, the name evident since it was inscribed in loopy cursive on the dusty back window of the family sedan compliments of Michaela, came to a halt behind the tumbledown fence.

"Some houses have a name in parts of Europe," Addie started as they piled out of the car. "Casa de Benitza would be a home in the Benitza family. Then, there's Roald Dahl's Gipsy House. Some people here in the United States name their houses, too."

"Can we name this house?"

Traffic whished by, down the highway that looped through town and separated them from the mountain, as Tim perched himself on the water meter and peeked over the fence. "It's unlocked," he announced.

Michaela and Addie strode over, careful to step around the thorny arms of young mesquite bushes. "Sure we can. It'll be like naming the puppy I want to get you for Christmas, only better. Do you have any ideas?"

Michaela giggled. "You mean the puppy you'll get *you* for Christmas?"

Addie shrugged and swept her brown bangs out of her thick fringe of lashes that seemed to always catch hold of them at the wrong time. "If we're going to have a big yard, we need a fat little puppy. Just sayin'."

"I agree." Michaela leaned down and plucked a bright yellow wildflower from those that blanketed the empty lot between the house and the alley. It smelled strangely citrus, with a touch of dill. Addie accepted it and stuck it in her hair.

"How about something French. For the house name, I mean. We have to see the puppy before we can name it."

Adelaide ignored the chills that danced down her spine and produced her phone from the back pocket of her jeans. The translator app was still pulled up. She began to type. "I think that's a fine idea. Maybe something like *Chez Nous*. That means Our Home. Or how about *Belle Vue* for Beautiful View? That certainly fits with the mountain right there." She looked at Michaela, who seemed lost in thought. "Do you have anything in mind?"

"Yup."

Tim worked the gate with a stick until finally it pushed inward.

Michaela tilted her face to look at her mother. "*Maison de Folie.*"

Addie sounded out the words carefully and typed them into the app. The smile faded from her lips as Michaela hurried ahead to catch up with her father, who had already disappeared into the picturesque backyard. Cold stones fell in her gut.

Maison de Folie—House of Madness.

Addie glanced over her shoulder at the mountain, looming and ever-present. She shook off the uneasiness and trotted through the open gate.

The pair of cardinals she'd seen from the bathroom window flitted overhead in the uppermost branches of a towering pine. All kinds of trees lined the fence from the inside. Addie recognized the weeping willow, soapberry, and the pines, but others were a mystery to her. Clumps of mistletoe clung to more than a few branches and tweeting birds sang from everywhere. She drew in a deep, slow breath.

Relax, Adelaide. This is going to be home.

Tim and Michaela surveyed the gentle slopes, probably trying to decide where to put Michaela's enormous trampoline. Or a doghouse. A stone bench sat beneath the cardinal's pine tree, so Addie sank down upon it. Her gaze found its way to the house.

From where she sat, the glittery dining room sparkled through the windows with a regal air. The walls of windows would be such a nice change from their cramped two-bedroom in Dallas. Everything they owned was packed neatly away and stacked in the back of their moving trailer at the motel. Addie pondered on this a moment. If she was to fill out a paper right now, she supposed they would be classified as situationally homeless.

She fought back a smile. *Like a Gypsy.*

A shadow of movement caught her eye. The picture window in the odd bathroom. She shielded her eyes and looked again.

Did someone walk in front of the window?

Addie glanced into the sky. Thick clouds, heavy with rain, dotted the sky around the sun. It was probably just—

"Mom, look!" Michaela dashed up the sloping hill with Tim right behind her. "In that shrub over there," she huffed, "is a dove nest. Three little eggs in it. Cool, huh Mom!"

"Very cool." *We'll need to hang bird feeders, for sure. Maybe Michaela and I can gather some pine cones and make some peanut butter and birdseed feeders once we get moved in.*

Tim checked his watch. The dappled shade accented all his features that she loved. Muscled arms. Angular jaw. Softly stubbled face. Strong calves. "It's time to head to the office and sign the papers."

Addie fidgeted with her loose ponytail. "Did we offer full price?"

Tim looked thoughtful a moment, his hazel eyes wide. "Actually, Kim said the kids were anxious to get rid of this place and to just make an offer. As a joke, I said about fifty thousand less than asking. Kim just nodded and made a note in her phone." He shrugged. "I guess we'll see in a few minutes."

Michaela perched on the stone bench next to Addie. "Hey, wasn't that light off when we left?"

The trio shifted their gazes back to the house in silence. Sure enough, a light shone from the secluded bathroom.

"Didn't Miss Kim turn that off Mom?"

Ice ran through Addie's veins. She stood. "Yes. She did."

Tim cupped his chin in his hand. "Hmm, we may need to ask about the electrical wiring then. Must be a short." He turned back to his family with a smile. "Ready to go buy a house?"

Addie and Michaela trudged back to the car while Tim locked the gate from the inside then climbed over. Despite feeling like she needed to, Addie did not turn around.

CHAPTER THREE

Maison de Folie

"First things first." Tim set the last of the "this side up" moving boxes, upside down of course, on the pink flagstone tile in the glittering dining room. Everything had gone more smoothly (and less expensively) than expected with Pink Kim the Realtor, and moving day was proving to be a success.

The rays of the setting sun caught the sparkles in the brown paint in such a way that Addie was sure this was how the old gold miners felt at Sutter's Mill. *In a way, Tim, Michaela and I struck gold, too.*

"Now that the U-Haul is unpacked," Tim continued, "there's something we have to do before we help Mom set up her writing room."

Addie flushed and sank down onto one of the black dining room chairs and swept her brown mane into a messy ponytail. A sheen of moving day sweat made her neck itchy. "I can't believe we actually have enough room to give me a writing room. No, writing nook." She wrinkled her nose at her husband. "It sounds more author-ish."

"Coming," Michaela called as she wheeled in her suitcase, the very last object from the back of the car and shut the front door with her foot. "I just can't get used to that smell. It's like Old Spice on steroids."

Addie offered her a sympathetic look through the open pass-throughs. "Come here Kiddo, Dad has a job for us."

Michaela stopped in the doorway. Her already sullen face fell further. "*Another* job?"

"Yup."

Michaela stared down the dark hallway. "But I really want to get my room set up."

"After this." Tim looked pointedly at his watch. "In exactly thirty seconds, your mom had better find a hiding place. Because the sun's going down and this is the best house for hide-and-seek in the history of the world. Ready Mack?"

Michaela squealed and began to count while peeking through wide fingers. "One ..."

Addie sprang to her feet. "Hide your eyes, both of you!"

"Two ... three ..."

She thought fast and ran past Michaela, who still wasn't hiding her eyes very well, and ducked behind the fifteen-mile-long breakfast bar.

Geez, that Old Spice smell is strong enough to gag a maggot.

"Twelve ... thirteen ... fourteen ..."

"Hey, you skipped some numbers in there," Adelaide called.

Michaela cackled. "Mom, you can't talk! Now we know where you are!"

Addie crawled along the fashionably cracked tile flooring toward the pantry. "You were peeking, you already knew," she laughed.

"Twenty ... twenty-one ... twenty-two ..."

She eased the thin doors open and pushed out the shelving.

The perfect hiding place.

Addie eased herself into the dark space and thought hard about wide open spaces and lots of sky. Careful to be quiet, she reached out and pulled shut the doors. Once she was concealed, Addie pulled the pantry shelves back into place.

A fat bead of sweat made its epic descent down her backbone, leaving a tickle in its wake. She swiped at her throat and forced a swallow.

The walls are not closing in. This is the perfect hiding place. It's just a room in my very own house …

A cabinet door creaked open and slammed, just outside her hiding spot. Addie jumped.

Come on Macky, I'm not in there. Look in here.

Another cabinet door creaked, then slammed. Followed by another.

Creak, *slam.* Creak, *slam.*

Does she really think I'm little enough to fit in there?

Addie nudged the shelving out of the way and ignored the tremble in her hands. "Michaela," she called as she pushed open the tall doors. "Do you really have to slam—"

Addie stopped in mid-sentence. The light flooded into her award-worthy hiding spot as she surveyed the kitchen. "Um, Macky?"

Addie stepped out. Several cabinet doors stood open, but neither Michaela nor Tim were there. She licked her lips and willed her racing pulse to calm.

"Ahh," Michaela shrieked as she ran full speed down the hall. "Found you, Mom!"

"You know," Tim added as he appeared behind her. "The object of the game is to *hide* and be found. Not stand in the middle of the kitchen until we make it in here to look for you."

Addie rolled her eyes and shook her head. "Hardy har har."

"Yeah," Michaela added. "And I know the house is big and everything, but when you start banging cabinet doors, it kind of takes the fun out of the game. We knew right where you were."

Addie opened her mouth to protest. "Slamming cabinet doors? But I thought you—"

Tim waved his arm wide. "Come on," he interrupted. "Back to the starting point in the glittery room. Since Mom is obviously still learning, let's let her hide one more time."

"Fine," Addie smiled. "But you two have to learn how to count this time, too."

"Deal," Macky and Tim said in unison. "One ... two ... three ..."

Addie snapped into action. She jumped over a small box and dashed down the dim hallway to the master bedroom. Tim's voice joined with Michaela's and echoed off the concrete walls.

"Nine ... ten ... eleven ..."

Addie's heart pounded as she flicked the switch in her bedroom. The fan spun slowly to life. *No lights in here? I hadn't realized that.*

She eased past the mattresses Tim had propped against the wall and stepped through the dressing area.

Ah, the bathroom.

Of course, the light was on.

Surely I can fit in one of these little storage places.

Addie pulled open door after door on the half-wall. Though each seemed to be a custom size, she would be hard pressed to shove herself in there and successfully close the door behind her. And keep her sanity.

Tim and Michaela's voices had taken on a slight chant, as though they were cheering the home team on to victory at a Friday night football game.

Seven-teen ... *eigh*-teen ... *nine*-teen ... *twenty!*

Addie's hand came to rest on the knob of the pull-out hamper Michaela had discovered the day they first explored the house. She hesitated. Her fingers tightened around the silver handle and her breathing came faster. It was bigger than it looked.

I could fit in here.

She gave the handle a tug. A whiff of musty air slapped her in the face. She reached behind her and shut off the light. Addie swallowed back a gag and set one foot inside. Her heartbeat quickened from a gentle, rhythmic thud to a smacking gallop against the inside of her chest.

Stop it, Addie. There is absolutely nothing to be afraid of. A small space for a few seconds won't kill you.

Still, she bit her lip and lifted her other leg inside. Every fiber of her being urged her to leap from the musty hamper and flee the room.

Don't be ridiculous.

"Ready or not, here we come!"

Her palms dampened as she squatted into the hamper. Ever slow, Addie leaned back to ease it shut. Michaela's sandal-clad feet slapped the flagstone tile.

Do it for your baby. Get over this stupid fear. Don't be the reason she doesn't have fun on the first night in the new house.

An odd sound met her ears. Addie stopped the hamper from closing and listened. Tim's cackling and Michaela's squealing sounded years away. She listened hard. Heavy breathing sucked in air and exhaled again quickly, punctuating the blackness with thick puffs. Terror, the kind that appears just before hysteria takes over, darkly muffled the sound from whoever made it. Addie froze in the stench of the hamper.

The breathing sound came faster in a steady crescendo, so close that she could almost feel the hot breath on her ear.

Is this my imagination? Yes, she answered. *Claustrophobia. It is my imagination. It is my imagination.*

Her fingers began to push back against the hamper door before it could seal shut. Gentle at first, almost politely. Politeness had always been her biggest asset. And her biggest flaw.

Fear shook her brain in tune with the huffing breath. So much that horrid memories, tucked neatly away in the dank corners of her mind, came rattling out like dice from a cup. In an instant, she was transported to that exact moment in time. The one she tried to forget more and more each day.

The morning had dawned bright. She could almost see it now, painfully clear through her closed eyelids. A day full of sunshine, full of hope. Adelaide rested her hand on the slight curve of her belly. She'd felt the flutters of life only a few days before. The sonogram confirmed she was, in fact, carrying another girl.

A baby sister for Michaela.

"It's going to be a gorgeous day, Little Grub," Addie whispered to the life growing inside her.

"Mommy!"

In all her seven-year-old zeal, Michaela dashed into her parent's cramped Dallas bedroom like an Olympic sprinter. She hurdled the pile of laundry that sat on the floor, patiently waiting for its turn in the washer today, and dodged her mother's oversized antique trunk that jutted out just a bit from the wall.

With her head still resting on her pillow, Addie held out her arms to her precious daughter.

Michaela, having awakened in a silly mood, grinned a

gapped-tooth grin and held out her arms as she ran. "Mom-m-m-m-y!" she bellowed.

Before she could leap to the safety of her mother's waiting arms, just as she'd done a hundred mornings before, Michaela's foot caught the bunched-up rug. Her young eyes widened as she fell, too hard and too fast.

Addie tried to scoot back, but her mind was working ahead of her body. Michaela's head hit hard, squarely on her mother's swollen belly.

Michaela's grunt was muffled by the covers. "Umph."

A stabbing pain in Addie's gut made a gasp strangle in her throat.

Oh no.

"Sor-wy Mommy," she mumbled. "Ow-chie."

A hot wetness dampened the inside of Adelaide's thighs as though her cotton underwear beneath her happy-puppy nightgown, as though they weren't even there.

Michaela raised up. "My nose is bweeding," she confirmed.

"Pinch it and tilt—ahh!" Addie squeezed into the fetal position as another savage cramp threatened to break her in two. "Go get my phone. Call Daddy."

It happened on the way to the Emergency Room.

Michaela sat in the backseat with the happy, electronic tune of her Nintendo breaking the uneasy silence as Tim drove too fast to Dallas Methodist. Addie sat on her hip in the passenger seat, with her legs pulled up to her chest. Her favorite nightgown was splotched with blood and sweat trickled down her cheeks. Or maybe they were tears.

The cramp came as Tim ground to a halt at the stop sign by Dunkin' Donuts. As the warm, sweet smell of the sugary pastries filled the car, Addie knew her pregnancy was over.

Doubled over in the seat, she reached between her legs with shaking hands. Something was there that shouldn't be.

"Tim!" Her voice was much too high pitched to be her own. "Oh, Tim." The remnants of their baby, still attached to her by the snakelike umbilical cord, filled her hand.

Tim cut his eyes to the baby, then quickly focused back on the road. He pushed the pedal down to the floor and took off with a rubber-stenched squeal. "Is she breathing?"

Leave it to Tim to be so matter-of-fact at a time when facts just wouldn't do.

Baby Juliette, small enough to fit in just one hand, was long and thin. Her tiny ankles were crossed, just as Michaela crossed hers whenever she wasn't thinking about it. Her doll-like hands were pressed together beneath her little chin, as if in prayer.

Addie's sobs came so hard and fast, that she almost dropped the slippery remains of their infant. "She's dead, Tim. She's black, her body is black. She's dead!"

Tim banged the steering wheel and blew through a red light. "I said, is she breathing!"

Somehow, he hit the radio button and Toto's *Hold the Line* burst to life over the speakers, reminding Addie that love wasn't always on time.

"No," Addie shrieked back.

Michaela's own cries harmonized with the sudden cacophony. "No no! Please God, no! I killed my sister, no please—"

"Breathe for her." Tim commanded. "Dammit Addie, do it now!"

Even though they were in the car, her world began to close in. Blackness ringed her watery vision and everything began to waver.

Addie slumped in her seat and willed the sudden burning that flamed her skin to cool.

I'm going to pass out.

"Adelaide!"

Addie shook her head and lifted Juliette to her lips. Her frail body was like ice. Ever careful, she covered her tiny mouth and nose with her mouth and blew. Another cramp doubled her over as her body discharged the placenta. It wasn't needed anymore.

"Again!"

Addie jumped. A smattering of tears dripped from her lashes and fell on the waxy skin of her dead baby.

Their tires ground to a halt and Tim laid on the horn. It sounded so far away. Red and blue lights flashed somewhere and Addie knew they were at the hospital. When the nurses in white flung open her door, Addie realized she didn't know who was screaming louder, her or Michaela.

Still, the music played on, with Bobby Kimbell commanding her to *Hold the line.*

"It wasn't the little girl's fault," the doctors echoed. They may as well have been robots. Emotionless. Faceless. "That little bit of a bump couldn't have aborted a pregnancy as far along as yours."

Their well-meaning words brought her no comfort.

When they disappeared, going on their way to different patients before going home to their perfect families, only a nurse was left in Addie's room. "It was already going to happen. God's will, if you believe in that sort of thing."

Addie remembered how the nurse, Sarah, stood by the bed, sucking on a lollipop as though life would go on.

Was she really sucking on a lollipop? Am I misremembering?

Somehow, Addie was out of the hamper and on the floor of the pink and blue bathroom. The light was on and the crying—oh, the crying. Loud, painful wails that seemed to be filled with fear and dread.

That doesn't sound like me. Am I making that noise?

"Mom? Oh Mom. Dad!" Michaela fell on the floor beside her. "Mom, are you okay?"

The cries seemed to quiet when Tim joined them. "Honey?"

Addie had her hand over her ears. "The crying, make it stop."

"Adelaide!" Tim pulled Addie's hands from her ears and wrested her into his lap like a child. "There's no crying. None. There are no sounds."

"Yeah," Michaela agreed. "The light just came on and that's how I found you."

Michaela paused a moment. "I guess you had the perfect hiding spot. I'd been in here once looking for you when the light was still off."

Sure enough, Tim was right. The crying had stopped. Addie opened her eyes. Michaela's beautiful heart-shaped face came into focus. Tim's chest was strong and warm. She sucked in a shuddering breath.

"Michaela," Tim whispered, "go push the mattresses down for me. They're propped up against the wall there. I'm going to help Mom to bed, okay?"

"Can I go unpack my room when I'm done?"

"Yes. If you're not scared to go all the way to the back of the house by yourself."

"Seriously?" Michaela clucked. "Of course I'm not scared."

Exhaustion clung to Addie's bones as she lay in the fetal position in the middle of the California king. Tim snuggled up behind her and pulled their thick blue comforter over both of them. "Are you okay, Addie?"

For once, she didn't hesitate or dance around with the usual *I'm fine* or *yes* or *what makes you think that.* "No Tim, I'm not. I'm not okay."

"You're just tired. It's been stressful. What with the move, and with looking for a teaching job if your book doesn't sell and all?" He nuzzled her hair. "And it will, Addie. ***A Heart on Hold*** is a great book. Tomorrow I'll get your writing nook all set up, so you can start on book two in the series. What's the title going to be again?"

"***A Heart Broken***," Addie sniffed.

Art imitating irony.

Talking about books, something she could normally do all day, just wasn't what was on her heart tonight. "It's not the tiredness, Tim. It just all happened so fast. Could I have done something different?"

Emotion clogged her throat.

Tim rubbed her back. "How about going to see someone? Like we talked about?"

"You think I'm crazy, don't you?"

The sounds of the new house were amplified in the silent dark. The overhead fan whipped the air like an airplane rotor and gave their room more the feel of a hotel than an actual house. Water heaters, air conditioners—normal little noises she hadn't had the chance to get used to yet—creaked and groaned like unwelcome guests overstaying their visit.

Cars zipped down the highway, their lights casting an eerie glow on the far wall of the curtainless bedroom wall. Like two glowing yellow eyes seeking and searching, but finding nothing, moving silently along their way into the blackness.

"Tim?"

"Hmm?"

"You didn't answer me."

Tim adjusted on the mattress, a sure sign he was in uncomfortable territory. "Addie, I think what happened—well, it's over. We just need to move on from it."

"You're dodging."

He exhaled loudly and turned completely on his back. The half-inch between them, where their bodies were touching just moments before, felt more like a mile. "I think you should talk to someone, yes. Something isn't right."

Addie buried her face in her hands. She wanted to cry. She wanted to let the cleansing tears soak her cheeks and leave their salty streaks as a reminder of the pain in her heart that refused to heal. A badge of her emotion. Perhaps even a sign that she was healing, that she was moving on. Accepting the pain, dealing with it. Thinking. Remembering.

But those tears just wouldn't come.

CHAPTER FOUR

Sprinkle Donuts and Fruit Loops

Addie didn't think she would ever get to sleep, but somehow she did. She must have, because the phone ringing pulled her from a dreamless slumber.

"Get the phone," she called.

Exhaustion reduced her voice to little more than a croak. But, as it sometimes happened, she had only been yelling in her dream. Still, the blasted thing kept ringing.

Addie forced her eyes open. Pale yellow fingers of sunlight stretched across their blue comforter, giving the room an early morning glow. Once upon a time, it had been Addie's favorite time of day. Now, it was much too bright. She kicked free of the tangled blanket. "First thing today, hang some curtains," she muttered.

Stepping over boxes and through tiny walkways lined with moving boxes, Addie finally made it to the kitchen. "Where is the ringing coming from?" She cleared her throat. "Tim? Honey?"

A piece of folded paper on the cabinet caught her eye.

Gone for donuts. Be back soon. Michaela's up, didn't want to go.

Adelaide's stomach leapt at the mention of donuts. The sweet, warm smell took her back to the day in the car. The same hellish day that she was never going to be able to put to rest. She dropped the note, face down on the marble counter.

"Where did you put the landline," Addie grumbled. Now, the ringing sounded as though it came from an entirely different part of the house. "I guess cement walls throw sound," she reasoned.

Through the living room, through the den, through her future writing nook. By the time she got outside of Michaela's closed door, the ringing stopped. Addie stood in the dim hallway in yesterday's rumpled clothes and ran her fingers through her tangled hair. "You have got to be kidding me."

A shrill giggle came from the other side of the door. Addie stepped closer and raised her hand to knock but stopped. Instead, she did something she'd never done before. Taking care to be quiet, she pressed her ear against her daughter's bedroom door—and listened.

Michaela's voice was muffled.

She must be back in the closet.

Addie listened harder. A family of birds flitted and chirped, sounding as though they had made a home in the chimney. The air conditioner kicked on. More mumbling from the other side of the door.

"*Mon nom est* Michaela."

Finally, something I can understand.

Addie pulled her phone out of her wind pants pocket, where it had apparently spent the night, and opened up the translator app. Careful not to hit the door, she typed in the words.

My name is Michaela.

"*J'ai onze ans.*" Clear all text. Type it in.

I am eleven years. Icy shudders tickled her backbone.

"*Et toi?*" Clear all text.

Damn, I closed the app.

Addie hit the app icon on her iPhone again. No luck. Try as she might, the app refused to open. Addie held down the power and the home buttons and did a hard reset on her phone. The single red bar threatened her with a low battery warning.

Why am I so nervous? It's not like she's really talking to someone in there. All kids have imaginary friends.

Addie studied the hidden purple door that opened to the front yard while she waited to see if her phone would come back to life. Thankfully, the screen lit up a few seconds later. The door looked to be locked.

Okay, time to translate.

She clicked the app icon again. This time, it opened without a hitch.

Addie was so intent on her phone, that she almost failed to notice the silence from the other side of the closed bedroom door.

Et trois, Addie mouthed. Was that what was said? *And three?*

No, something wasn't right in her spelling.

Et toi. Ah, yes. That's it.

Addie's fingers froze when the translation popped up on the English side of the screen. *And you?*

Something metallic slammed behind her. A scream tore from her throat without warning. Michaela's door banged open. "Mom? Mom! What are you doing?"

Addie's heart thundered in her chest. "Did you hear that? That bang?"

Dark, tired circles made Michaela's face look gaunt and tired. "I heard you scream. Right outside my door." She narrowed her big blue eyes. "What were you doing there, anyway?"

Addie tucked her phone back into her pocket and opened her mouth to speak.

"Well—"

"I'm ho-ome!" Tim sounded like a sportscaster. "Who wants do-o-onuts?"

Addie forced her open mouth in to a smile. "Come on, let's have some breakfast."

Michaela furrowed her thick brows. "Um, okay. I'll be there in a minute." She strode back into her room and closed the door without looking back.

"We'll be in the kitchen," Addie called through the door.

No response.

The hot, sugary scent led Addie to where Tim was arranging the dining room table. "Well hello Sleeping Beauty," he quipped with a smile. Apparently last night's conversation was forgotten.

Or ignored.

Tim dragged his hand across his forehead. In his faded gray UT Arlington shirt and jeans, Addie was sure he'd never looked more handsome.

I can ignore it if he can.

He pushed the last of the four black chairs into place.

She strode across the room and wrapped her arms around his waist. "Good morning."

"I set up the table for you. Maybe it will feel more like home." He offered a hopeful smile.

Together, they studied the room. Their marble-topped table sat in the middle of the golden den, looking exquisite beneath the cut glass chandelier.

Seating for four. But just three bodies to fill the chairs. Almost perfect.

"Wow," Addie breathed. "It looks like this room was made for this table, doesn't it?"

Tim smiled down at her. "You look beautiful surrounded by sparkles."

A creeping blush burned up Addie's neck and into her cheeks. She pushed herself up on her tiptoes and pressed her lips to his. "Thank you. For everything."

He squeezed her tighter. "I love you, Addie. We're in this together, okay?"

Addie nodded. "Oh, and you'll have to show me where you plugged in the landline phone later. I couldn't find it earlier."

Tim loosened his hug and motioned to one of the chairs. Ever the gentleman, he pulled it out for her. However, the look on his face made something in her stomach turn.

Tim flipped open the donut box and took the seat across from her. "Say what?"

Addie stared into the box. A year before, she could have polished off the box of donuts by herself. Not anymore.

"The phone." Her voice sounded meek, even to her own ears. "Thanks for plugging it in. But when it was ringing and ringing this morning, I couldn't find it to answer it."

Michaela padded into the room with bare feet. "Mmm, donuts. Did you get the kind with the tiny round sprinkles Dad? You know I can't eat any other kind of sprinkles."

Tim forced a chuckle. "Of course, Your Majesty." He was trying much too hard to keep the mood light. "The long sprinkles are too thick."

"And the colors aren't right," Adelaide echoed. Michaela had a thing about textures and colors, especially with her food.

Tim slid out the chair next to him. "Have a seat, sweetie."

Her face stoic, Michaela perched in her chair like a tall,

blonde bird. Her hair hung straight, well past her shoulders. Despite claiming to be happy to have gotten the house, she hadn't smiled once since they moved in. "Thank you."

Addie watched as Michaela meticulously studied each donut. After a full minute, she chose the one with the most evenly-distributed tiny, round, vivid sprinkles.

She'd always known Michaela was special, even from the day she gave birth to her in the hospital. Everybody in the room thought so, especially since she was born with a caul over her face. However, denial is a heavy drug. It wasn't until the afternoon that her preschool teacher called home that Addie let her suspicions be confirmed.

"Mrs. Smithfield?"

Addie could hear a baby wailing in the background. She'd been studying for her TExES teacher exam when the phone rang. Early Childhood through Sixth Grade, generalist. When this test was passed, she would be a real, certified teacher. She pushed the manuals to the back of her desk and sat at attention. "Yes, this is she."

The voice of a shrieking child screeched through the phone. An adult voice calmly spoke over it. "This is Miss Preston, Michaela's teacher."

Addie plucked up her car keys and started toward the door, almost tipping the dining room chair, which doubled as her desk chair, in the process. "What's wrong? Is that Michaela in the background?"

"Yes, it is. We had Fruit Loop cereal for a snack," she explained. "There's no need for concern, really, but I thought you should hear her reaction—"

"Reaction?"

Miss Preston must have stepped from the room because Michaela's crying ceased. "She didn't eat. Instead, she spent all of snack time lining up the pieces of cereal by color. In concentric circles."

She paused, as though to drive her point home. "She did it perfectly, by the color of the rainbow. Red on the outside, orange next. Followed by yellow, green, blue, and then purple. Which we haven't learned yet." Miss Preston took a deep breath and let it out slow. "Michaela is extremely sweet, Mrs. Smithfield. Sweet as I've ever seen. And so smart."

But.

"But, when it was time to clean up, I picked up her bowl. And she lost it."

"She threw a fit then." Addie chewed her lip. "She couldn't eat them until every last piece was in order, right?"

"Right." Miss Preston breathed a sigh. Probably of relief. "Well, I really don't think it was a fit. I think it was more of a meltdown."

Addie placed the keys back in the key bowl on the counter. "Is there a difference?"

"Yes. Kids throw a fit when they don't get what they want. Perhaps they've been a little bit spoiled."

Stones fell in Addie's gut. Cold, hard stones. And Miss Preston was the one throwing them with her words.

"Miss Smithfield, if a child has a meltdown, it means they can't process what's happening in their environment. They're overstimulated, they're not spoiled. They simply can't express their emotions in any other way. Like what we had here today."

Addie sank onto a barstool. "Miss Preston, why would a student have a meltdown?"

"Well, as I said. Tantrums or fits come from students who may be a bit spoiled. Meltdowns are a different animal all together."

Addie held on to that moment of ignorance as hard as she could. Just those few seconds of silence really were a gift. The not knowing. Whatever Miss Preston said next, whatever label they associated with Michaela, would follow her for the rest of her life.

"Meltdowns, more often than not, signify an underlying problem. No, not problem. Excuse me. A condition. Recently, they gave it a name. It is on the autism spectrum. It's called Asperger's syndrome."

Addie's memory faded as she stared at her daughter as she carefully went through the motions of choosing a second donut. "Mom, did you hear me?"

She shook her head. "I'm sorry baby, I guess I was daydreaming."

Tim stared hard across the table. "She asked if Ritchie was the name of a bad guy."

Michaela's questions. Always off the wall and always random. The summer between second and third grade, she and Tim had decided to put her in a summer day camp. It had gone fairly well, until a month after the camp ended. One morning, out of nowhere, Michaela surfaced at the foot of their bed well before sunrise.

Addie had fallen asleep with her reading light on, so her side of the bedroom was illuminated in the pre-dawn darkness with an ethereal glow. She jumped when Michaela moved.

"Macky? What are you doing?" Addie rubbed her eyes and

squinted at the digital clock on the bedside table. "It's five in the morning. You have two and a half more hours to sleep before we have to get up and ready for the day."

"Mommy I had to come tell you something."

Addie sat up and patted the bed between her and Tim, who managed to sleep through every crisis. "What is it?"

Michaela's face was stoic as she climbed on the bed and slipped between the covers. "I had to tell you. Never, ever make me hot dogs again. Okay?"

Adelaide's jaw went slack. "Um, okay. Why the sudden hatred of all things hot dog?"

Michaela stared at her as though they were discussing something where life and death hung in the balance. "Because at camp, Julian put his nose on my arm during lunch. Now, every time I eat a hot dog, it tastes like noses."

Addie closed her eyes for a moment, but pretended it was just for a yawn. "Let me guess. You were having hot dogs when Julian put his nose on your arm?"

Michaela exhaled hard. "No." She was getting frustrated. "No Mother. We were *talking* about hot dogs while we ate cheese enchiladas."

"Ah, I understand." She gave her daughter a squeeze. "Do you want to lay down in here with me and Daddy?"

"No." Michaela inched down to the end of the bed and slid off the comforter. She walked to the door and didn't look back until she reached the doorway. "Mommy?"

"Yes?"

"Since you said that, don't ever make me cheese enchiladas again either, okay? They'll taste like hot dogs."

"Mother!"

Addie shook her head. "Sorry, Mack. I didn't sleep well last night. What?"

"Are all Ritchie's bad people?"

"I suppose it would depend on the person."

Addie's stomach rumbled. A couple of donuts were left in the box. Neither had equally dispersed sprinkles, so it's not like Michaela would be eating one. Addie took a deep breath and chose the most smashed of the two before she continued.

Time to put the past to rest. Time to be normal.

Addie chewed the pastry and swallowed the bite. It tasted like sawdust. "Do you think Ritchie is the name of a bad guy?"

Michaela nodded. "Ritchie is mean. I don't like anyone named Ritchie."

Adelaide said a mental prayer for any of Michaela's future classmates who had the bad luck to be named Ritchie.

Michaela folded her paper towel in half, then in half again. "Ritchies slam doors. And they don't like dogs."

Addie glanced at Tim. *He must think he's the only one among us who has a mind that operates halfway decent.*

"Well baby, don't judge all Ritchie's just from one."

Michaela shrugged and stacked the pepper shaker on top of the salt. "I don't know. You've always said anyone that doesn't like dogs can't be trusted any further than you could throw them. And I don't think I could throw Ritchie very far."

Addie tried to conceal a laugh, but it escaped anyway as a snort. Sometimes, Michaela's thought process was so entirely off the wall that it came full circle and made a bit of sense.

Tim, however, wasn't laughing at all. "Who is Ritchie, Mack? Someone in one of your classes at school last year or something?"

Mack stared at her dad. A deadpan stare that had proven

to give parents of non-autistic children the creeps. "Ritchie gets mad. He likes to slam things."

An icy breeze brought goosebumps to Addie's arms. She pushed back from the table with a scrape. "Well now. I was thinking of putting a fort together in that tree out front today. Want to help me?"

Mack shrugged again. "Maybe so. Thanks, Mom."

Tim grabbed the last donut out of the box as Adelaide picked it up from the table. "I'd like to help."

"Really? Thanks." Addie offered him a smile. "I look forward to it."

Michaela stood up. "Can I get back to my room now? I have a lot to unpack and put away."

Tim nodded. "Sure thing Kiddo. Hey, I'm proud of you for taking such responsibility over your room."

"Can I take the salt, too?"

"Um." Tim looked at Addie. "I ... guess?"

Michaela smiled, a bright and genuine smile. Finally. "Thanks Dad."

Addie stuffed the used paper towels into the donut box as Michaela left the room. "Tim, thanks for offering to help with a fort." She paused. "Oh, what did you knock down when you got home with breakfast?"

"Knock down?" Tim took the empty donut box and stuffed it into a black plastic trash bag on the floor. "I didn't knock anything down."

"That's odd." Addie took Tim's hand in hers. "I guess it was Ritchie."

Tim and Addie shared a laugh as they walked together through the dining room and into the kitchen. The Old Spice smell was still strong, right by the door.

"Ritchie," Addie called through her giggles, "we really wish you'd wear a different cologne!"

CHAPTER FIVE

RITCHIE

Michaela crept into her room and pushed the door shut as quietly as she could. The salt shaker was uncomfortable in her pocket. She wasn't sure why she had to bring it, but she did as she was asked.

"My friend?" Michaela whispered. "*Mon ami?*"

The closet door pushed outward.

"I've got the salt, just like you said." Michaela pulled the closet door open a bit more and stepped inside. "Why do you stay in here, Lisette?"

Lisette's voice had a thick French accent, even when she spoke English. "I'm scared of Ritchie. He won't come in here, though. That was him earlier, in the kitchen. The banging. He's mad." Lisette's voice met her ears like a warm summer breeze. "Look in the mirror."

Michaela sank down, crisscross-applesauce, in front of the mirror that hung on the inside of her closet door. Sure enough, Lisette's visage flickered to life behind her. Every time she appeared, she wore the same checkered dress that would have looked more at home on a prairie girl a hundred years ago.

"I'm not even scared of you," Michaela told the reflection of the girl with the thick black braids and paste white skin. "It's weird."

"I'm not scared of you, either. I hide from your *mamah* and *papa*, though."

Michaela rolled the salt shaker in her hands. "You don't have to be scared of them. They'd like you."

Lisette's imagine flickered as thought it was just a frame on an old-time movie reel. "I thought your *mamah* saw me once or twice. She's fun to watch. But your *papa*—"

"What about him?"

"Well, I don't think he'll ever see me."

"Oh." Michaela held up the salt. "Why did we need this?"

Lisette glanced around, as though she was making sure nobody was listening, then leaned toward the mirror. Something in her eyes wasn't quite human.

Michaela shivered.

"Ritchie lives in the attic. He is very mean." It looked like Lisette put her translucent hand on Michaela's shoulder. "Tonight, you and I are going to trap him in there."

Michaela tucked the salt into the corner of the closet. "You promised that if I brought salt, I could see your dog."

"I will go find him. Sometimes I think he gets lost." Lisette smiled into the mirror. "Go find all the salt you can and bring it. To trap a ghost, you lock him in with a line of salt. They can't get out until they count every single grain."

"I understand. I like to count things, too. Sometimes I can't keep on doing whatever I'm supposed to be doing until I finish counting things." Michaela smiled. "Maybe I'm part ghost."

"That could be," Lisette agreed. "Or maybe some ghosts are just part human."

Michaela stared into the mirror. "Lisette? Are you and Ritchie the only ghosts here?"

Lisette shook her head. "No."

Michaela shifted her weight on the floor. "Um, okay."

They sat in silence for a while before Michaela spoke again. "Lisette? Can I ask you something?"

"Oui."

She hesitated a moment. "What made you become a ghost?"

The little French girl quit moving and stared into the mirror at her. Then, as quickly as she'd come, she faded away. Michaela was alone again.

"What do you girls want for dinner?" Tim's called from the kitchen. "Pesto tortellini okay?"

Dad had set up Mom's writing nook and Mom was typing furiously in front of a glowing monitor.

Normally, she says hi whenever I go by. She must really be in the zone.

As she skipped through the living room, she let her hand drag along the top of the brown suede couch. Something about how it felt made her feel comfortable. *Mom and Dad had talked about leaving the living room set and just buying new. I'm sure glad they didn't.* She hopped off the living room carpet and onto the kitchen tile. "Sounds good, Dad. Can I help?"

Tim stood in front of the stove and stirred a pot of boiling water. "Sure Honey, pass me the box of pasta."

"Okay." Michaela picked up the box of cheese tortellini. "Did Mom work on my fort today?"

"I'm not sure baby." Tim turned the chicken that had begun to sizzle in the skillet. "She may be working on it now."

"Nope, she's writing right now." Michaela turned around. "Here you go, Dad."

As Tim stepped over to retrieve the box, one of the cabinet doors flew open and met his nose with a sickening smack.

Michaela's knees turned to water and she dropped the box of pasta. They scattered across the floor. "Ritchie."

Blood spurted from Tim's nose. "What the—"

Salt. I need salt.

Michaela jumped over the pieces of broken tortellini and skidded into the pantry door. She flung it open and pawed through the jars and canisters until she found the giant blue and white can of salt. She didn't bother to check on Tim or the burning chicken. Instead, she dashed all the way back to her room and slammed the door.

Stinking writer's block. Addie stepped out of the sunken shower in the far bathroom and flung a fluffy towel around her shoulders. An email had come through while she was working on a pivotal scene in **A Heart Broken**.

Charlotte, having just discovered she was pregnant, hadn't had a chance to tell Sanderson—who in fact had survived the Yankee prison by relying on his keen wit and a little luck— before the Army came knocking with an arrest warrant and list of trumped up charges. After Sanderson was carted off in chains and at gun point to stand trial for something he didn't do, Charlotte suffered a miscarriage.

Addie was just beginning to delve into the soul-crushing heartbreak in Charlotte's deep point of view, but the ding of the email interrupted her.

```
Re: Query and Synopsis for A HEART
ON HOLD
```

From: Yesteryear Literary Agency

Adelaide's heart leapt into her throat as she opened the email.

Dear Potential Yesteryear Author,
Thank you for considering Yesteryear
Literary Agency for representation
of your manuscript, (insert title
here).
While we know you have spent
countless hours creating this
manuscript, we regret to inform you
that none of our esteemed agents
here at Yesteryear Literary Agency
connected with your characters in
such a way that we feel we would do
your book justice in the world of
literary marketing.
However, we suggest taking writing
classes and continuing to hone
your craft in any way you are able.
Don't stop writing! We hope you
find an agent who is more adept at
representing titles like (insert
title here).
Sincerely,
Yesteryear Literary Team

They didn't even bother to insert the title. Stinkin' form letters.
Adelaide was no stranger to rejection. She knew once

she started sending *A Heart on Hold* out for consideration by publishers and agents, she would be told, *No.* However, apparent apathy was far more hurtful than outright *Thanks but no thanks.* Her muse fizzled to nothing as she read the email, so maybe a shower would help. The hot water and French Lavender soap did help soothe her hurt feelings a little bit.

Dang. I left my clothes in the dressing area by the pink bathroom. I hate going in there. She wrapped the towel around her body and tiptoed past Michaela's bedroom. It smelled like Tim was cooking dinner. Chicken and pasta, his favorite.

I'll get dressed and go give him a hand.

Addie strode through the master bedroom and into the dressing area. Sure enough, there were the clothes she'd hung up but forgot to grab before she went to shower. She tried not to look into the creepy bathroom.

Adelaide let the towel fall to the floor as she slipped her *Te Amo Taco Tuesday* shirt off the hanger and pulled it over her head. The memory of her favorite happy puppy nightgown, and how it looked covered in blood and crumpled in the hospital trash, gave her pause. She pushed the thought away, to the back of her mind where it wouldn't bother her anymore, and pulled on her black bike shorts.

Even if there was a shower in this pink and blue bathroom, I wouldn't use it.

She shivered. A flash of movement caught her eye and Adelaide froze. Against her better judgment, she stepped quietly into the bathroom where, of course, the light was on.

"Michaela," she whispered, taking care to keep her voice even. "Is that you?"

There was nobody beside the tub, which looked to be even

more exposed and alone than the last time she was in there. Still, Addie knew wasn't alone.

A hissing whisper from behind met her ears. "Ro-chelle-e-e."

Addie shook her head. The light flickered. She held tight to the hem of her Taco shirt and crept up to the half wall. She took a deep breath and held it. Summoning every ounce of courage that she wasn't too sure she possessed, Addie stepped to the other side of the wall. And screamed.

Tim ran into the room. He had his nose pinched and his head tilted back. Dried smears of blood covered his face and hands. "What's wrong Addie?"

"Oh, nothing," Addie said, forcing a smile. She unpeeled herself from the wall and took deep breaths to slow her breathing.

It was hideous. The figure of what was probably a woman—at some point in her life. A skeleton now, not a woman.

"I, um, saw a spider," Addie continued. She hoped Tim didn't pick up on the waver in her voice. "We might ought to call an exterminator."

The hair—long stringy black hair. Looked like handfuls had been ripped out. Bloody bald patches. And the face she was making.

"Everything's fine though. I'm sorry I gave you a start."

It hissed at me. Its name was Rochelle.

"Maybe we should get someone out to check on the light in here, too."

The mouth was open and the body shook, as though it was being electrocuted.

"But enough about that," Addie segued. She stepped past Tim and into the dressing area. "What happened to you?"

Tim unpinched his nose. A fresh stream of blood trickled down over his lip. Addie pinched it for him again, hard. "I was cooking dinner," Tim said in nasal tones. "I guess left a cabinet door open and I ran smack-dab into it. Funny though, I don't remember opening anything. Haven't even put anything up there in those cabinets yet."

Tim covered Addie's hand with his and took it off his nose. He didn't let go but held it. This time, blood didn't trickle. "Quirky house we got, isn't it? No wonder we could afford it."

"Oh, that reminds me." Addie let herself be led out of the dressing room. "Can you flick off the light, Tim?"

He reached behind him and hit the switch without looking back. "What did you remember?"

"Pink Kim the Realtor texted me today. Apparently, both of the doctors who owned this place are going to be in town. Soon. And want to meet us. Told me they would be coming by sometime."

The smell of burnt chicken was strong when they stepped out of their bedroom.

"I guess the smoke detectors don't work." Addie giggled.

Maybe I just imagined the whole thing in the bathroom—

Tim raised her hand to his lips and brushed it with a dry kiss. "Let's go out for dinner. There's a pizza place around the corner." He smiled. "After I get cleaned up, of course."

"It's a date, Mister Smithfield. Oh, and I left Michaela some of those chewy hot candies she likes on the counter. Will be a nice surprise for her to find in the morning."

"Do you have the salt?" Lisette stared intently into the mirror. Her eyes were wider and brighter than normal tonight. "All of the salt you could find?"

Michaela nodded. "I do. I got all the salt I could find, and the sugar, too." She produced the five-pound bag. "I mean, sugar looks like salt, right? Maybe we can trick him?"

"Sugar is white, like salt?" Lisette's black brows knitted together over her eyes. "I've never seen it."

Michaela balked. "You've never tasted sugar?"

Lisette shook her head.

The bag of white sugar weighed heavy in Michaela's hands. She pursed her lips. "Can I try and help you taste it?"

Lisette's eyes were so dark they looked like empty sockets. "Is it good?"

Michaela pinched a bit of the precious white grains in between her thumb and pointer finger. "Oh yes, it is so good."

Lisette's expression was blank, then she nodded. "Yes. Let's try."

"Okay, here goes." Michaela lifted the bit of pinched sugar to the mirror. "Stick out your tongue."

Lisette did as Michaela instructed.

Slowly, Michaela rubbed her thumb and forefinger together. The white grains fell until they reached Lisette's tongue in the reflection, then they disappeared.

Michaela grinned. "Wow, that was cool."

Lisette worked her mouth over the foreign substance. Her face was contorted in such a way that Michaela could only describe it as thoughtful. A moment later, her mouth widened into a grin. "That was so good. I love sugar."

"Maybe if we gave Ritchie some sugar to try, he would be happier and then turn nicer." Michaela cocked her head. "Ya think?"

"No. I don't think so. But maybe it will trick him and he will have to count the grains, like the salt." Lisette flickered in the closet mirror, but her stoic expression was gone. She was smiling. "Thank you for the taste."

"You're welcome."

"Are you ready to trap a Ritchie?"

Michaela nodded.

Lisette was all business in her checkered prairie girl dress. "Are your parents asleep?"

Michaela nodded again.

"Mom stayed up writing for a while, but she is in bed now. Probably asleep, too."

"Yes, I saw her at the computer. I like watching her."

Michaela gave Lisette a quizical glance. "How do you know what a computer is?" she asked.

"I listened when your *mamah* talks," the spectre replied. "I like listening to your *mamah* talk."

A cold shudder rippled across Michaela's skin like tiny waves on a pond. She adjusted her weight on the hard closet floor. "That sounds kind of creepy, Lisette. That you watch people when they don't even know you're there."

Especially since it's my mom.

"Oh." Lisette's voice was small. "I like to be near her. She reminds me of my own *mamah*." Her small voice trailed off into the darkness until it was more of a thought than actual words. "I miss her so much."

"I didn't mean to hurt your feelings, if I did."

Lisette ignored the apology. "She was writing something tonight that made her cry. She read it out loud to herself. Something about a baby who died in the mother's tummy."

Michaela bit her lip. She didn't want to talk about such things tonight. Tonight was supposed to be about trapping a mean ghost. Not about bad memories.

Still, Lisette continued. "When she started crying, it made me want to cry. So I pushed a plant over and it spilled on the floor. She said 'Michaela, are you there?' She thought I was you."

They sat in silence, neither knowing what to say.

A moment later, Michaela broke the silence. "Why do you think she calls it writing, when she clearly isn't writing, she's typing?"

Lisette flickered in the mirror again, but her big eyes—strangely bright—were downcast.

Michaela gulped. "I'm sure you mother misses you, Lisette. Maybe she is waiting for you somewhere. Waiting until the right time to come get you." Michaela winced. She knew her explanation sounded simple and stupid when she said it out loud. "Any mother would be happy to have you for a baby girl."

Finally, Lisette looked at Michaela again. "Thank you, *mon ami*."

"Hey," Michaela said in a chipper tone. "Don't I get to see your dog, Dog?"

Lisette shook her head. "I couldn't find Dog. I'm sorry. But I'll show you him someday, I promise."

"Okay. Deal."

"Let's go trap a Ritchie."

Michaela pushed the closet door open. The darkness that filled the house was almost tangible. While nothing was out of the ordinary, per se, nothing felt right either. "It feels like when you walk into the room right after your parents had a fight," she whispered. "The air is heavy. And angry."

She couldn't see Lisette anymore, but she heard her words plainly. "That's Ritchie."

Michaela crept down the inky black hallway. She would

have preferred to follow Lisette, but since she couldn't see her, she made small talk instead. "Why is he so mad?"

"I don't know."

Michaela looked down the black hallway to her parents' bedroom. In the window reflection, she could see the bathroom light going off, on, off, on. Something tickled her spine when she turned her back on it and continued to the kitchen. "Why does their light do that Lisette?"

"The light doesn't do it. Rochelle does." Lisette's form was visible for a second beneath the silver moonlight as they crossed through the glittery dining room.

Phew, she's in front now.

"Is Rochelle nice, like you?"

Michaela sensed that Lisette stopped, so she stopped too.

"Rochelle scares me. But she's not mean. I think."

Michaela shuddered. "It seems like it's scarier to be a ghost than it is to be ..." She almost said *alive*, but she caught herself. Somehow, it seemed like it would come across as derogatory. "To be *not* a ghost," she finished. Michaela gave herself a mental pat on the back and puffed her chest as they continued to the play room.

"*Mon ami*, you are so right. It is very scary, that's why I hide in the closet." Lisette changed the subject. "Okay, we have to go up to the attic."

Tim's ladder was propped against the wall of the playroom. Right above it, was the attic entrance. "Dad thought squirrels lived in there."

Something skittered above them then *thunked* against the wall. Michaela flinched and fingers of fear tightened around her throat. She tried to swallow and almost choked.

"That's Ritchie," Lisette said. Her voice was edged in fear.

"Hurry, climb the ladder and dump the salt all around the entrance. Dump the sugar, too. I'll make sure he's still in there. We really don't want to lock him *out* of where he lives. Then he'd be *really* mad."

Michaela scampered halfway up the ladder with the salt shaker stuffed in her pocket and the big canister of salt tucked in the crook of her arm. She glanced through the playroom windows, straight into her parent's bedroom. The light flickered faster than ever. She shivered and almost dropped the canister.

Dang it, forgot the sugar. Michaela stopped. "Um, Lisette? What happens if Ritchie catches us?"

"You don't want to know, trust me." The moonlight shone through the play room windows and illuminated Lisette as she floated to the ceiling. "Ready? I'll say when."

Michaela tried to nod. Her head wouldn't really work. She hoped her legs would, when it was time to climb up the rest of the way. And especially when it was time to climb back down. Something knotted in her stomach and threatened to revolt. *Never in a million years did I think I'd be doing something like this. Didn't even think something like this was possible.*

"I don't see him, but I think he's in there. Go Michaela, go go go!" Lisette's voice was shrill, like an ambulance siren at its highest octave. "Go!"

Michaela's forced her feet to climb the last few steps. With her free hand, she pushed the attic door, just like she'd seen her father do. She didn't realize she'd closed her eyes until she opened them and looked around. The fact that it was blacker than night in the windowless crawlspace was both a blessing and a curse. With shaking hands, Michaela took the salt canister from the crook of her arm. She traced an imperfect circle around the hole and tossed the empty can into the attic. She stuck her hand in her pocket but fumbled the salt shaker. It clattered to the floor and grains fell across the pink tile in a white spray. "Dang!"

"Michaela, go back to our room now." Lisette's voice was far away, like she was already almost to the safety of the closet. "Hurry!"

Though she hadn't seen anything, a veil of cold sweat cloaked Michaela's face. Fear drove her down the ladder at record speed and down the hall to her room. The entire run seemed longer than normal, like she'd hit a time warp between the attic and her room, or the house elongated on its own. From the corner of her eye, the flickering light in her parent's bathroom was like a strobe light.

"Something's following me," Michaela hissed as she slid into her closet like a baseball player sliding into home. "You said we were safe here right? No ghosts, well no Ritchie ghosts, come here?"

Lisette didn't answer.

"Lisette?" Michaela stared into the mirror. Her friend was facing the wrong direction. The sight of Lisette's image with her back to her turned her blood to ice.

She swallowed her fear, but her voice still came out squeaky. "Are you okay?"

The Old Spice smell from the front door hung thick in the closet and threatened to suffocate her. "Ew, that smell is—"

An ominous figure loomed at the closet door. "You're wrong. To all the questions you asked. You're *dead* wrong."

It's Ritchie.

In the darkness of the closet, something growled. "Hush, Dog," Lisette scolded meekly.

"You're right to shut your dog up," Ritchie yelled. "I hate dogs!"

The energy in the dark room turned sinister. Across the room, the bookshelf her mom had painted for her last summer tipped and shook, sprinkling her beloved books on the floor like raindrops. Her bed jumped as though it was on springs. Drawers opened and shut with slams and bangs.

Michaela covered her ears. Mr. Henderson's face from second grade appeared in her mind. He liked to yell and pitch fits, too. Especially when she asked for help on math, her weakest subject. "Don't yell at me!"

The commotion in her room stopped, but Ritchie's massive frame still hulked, dark and shapeless and faceless, in the closet doorway.

Michaela pushed herself to her feet and tried to ignore her wobbly knees. "Why are you being so *ugly?*"

Lisette appeared beside her, albeit a little bit off behind her. Something whimpered from behind them both.

Dog.

Heavy breathing filled the cramped closet and surrounded them with a wretched cloud of stench. Finally, Ritchie spoke again. "I *hate* dogs."

"Why?" Michaela couldn't keep the honest words from flying off her tongue. "I would love to have a dog, but Dad says no, even though Mom says she thinks she can talk him into it by Christmas, with a little luck." Michaela crossed her arms. "Dog here is a good pet, too. Nobody here has hurt you."

Ritchie was silent.

Michaela leaned toward the phantom. "Have they?"

The mirror animated on the back of the door. The picture rolled for a few seconds, like an old black-and-white film.

When it stopped, men in Army uniforms filled the mirror that had transformed into a screen. There was no sound, only a grainy picture.

Sand dunes reached for the horizon in all directions and the men climbed into armored vehicles. One man in particular carried a large weapon.

"Is that you, Ritchie? In the Middle East?"

Ritchie's voice was low, like thunder through a distant canyon. "Yes. Desert Storm."

The vehicle rolled along through the desert landscape, almost like a coyote and roadrunner cartoon.

"What's Desert Storm?" Michaela whispered.

"War."

A massive explosion on the screen shook the room and a crack appeared along the top corner of her closet mirror. When the smoke and dust cleared, tall men with long guns and turbans on their heads swarmed down from the dunes, right on top of the overturned vehicle.

Michaela covered her mouth. Somewhere in the reflection, she saw Lisette's wide eyes watching intently.

The dark-skinned men in the white turbans pulled the soldiers out of the vehicle, which now had flames spurting from around the wheels, and laid them in a disheveled heap. The vehicle exploded and, in the background, a big soldier crawled to safety behind a sand dune. Another of the turbaned men dragged the soldiers out and laid them in a row. Michaela's stomach felt sick. She may not know much about Desert Storm, but she had been the best in her class at foreshadowing. "Oh no."

One tall man charged his weapon and shot the first soldier in line in the leg. He jerked. The same tall man then shot him in the head. He stepped over to the second soldier. Before he could squeeze off a shot, a burst of gunfire sprayed from behind the sand dune.

Michaela clapped before she could help herself. "Ritchie, is that you? Saving your friends?"

Three of the bad guys fell to the sand before the rest of them descended on Ritchie like fire ants on honey. The mirror faded to black.

Michaela's breath was coming hard and fast when a fresh scene opened on the cracked mirror. Now, they were in a camp of some sort. Barking dogs were everywhere as another lanky man in a turban whipped Ritchie with a chain.

"It's no wonder he doesn't like dogs then," Michaela whispered.

"Yeah," Lisette whispered. "I'm sorry to have Dog in here, Ritchie. But I promise, he won't hurt you. He would never hurt anyone. He is just a puppy."

Michaela stared at the screen. "Ritchie, you're about to give up and die, aren't you? I can sense it."

Ritchie was silent, but the face of a beautiful woman filled the mirror over the horrendous torture scene. Light colored hair was swept back from her face with youthful abandon and showcased her wide smile and sparkling eyes. A handful of freckles spangled her nose and cheeks. There were no words, but it was obvious that this woman was Ritchie's wife.

Another explosion rattled the mirror and furthered the crack in the corner, splintering it into a spiderweb of broken glass. The soundless memory-movie continued and showed Ritchie pulling himself up out of the rubble and running, yelling and waving his arms above his head.

He spoke again in his low, thundering voice. "They rescued me. Our forces. They didn't even know I was a prisoner there."

The woman's face appeared again, but her smile was notably absent. A dark shadow stood out beneath one eye. Ritchie's face, angry and contorted with rage, filled the mirror behind his wife. Lights flashed, like on a police car, and both faces disappeared.

Michaela followed along, her heart breaking a bit more with each subsequent scene.

The next scene showed an angry Ritchie, strapped down to a gurney with tubes stuck in his arms and attached to plastic bags on poles, being wheeled into a building beneath a giant sign that read Big Spring Sanatorium. Two old people stood in the doorway; a man and a woman. When they turned to follow him into the building, Michaela saw their names.

Dr. M. Darkland and Dr. R. Darkland. They shared a smile and the scene faded away.

"Oh Ritchie ..." Sympathy filled Michaela's very being to bursting.

Still, the hellish movie played on as if on its own accord. Michaela didn't figure that Ritchie could stop the horrific flood of memories now, even if he wanted to.

Inside the Big Spring Sanatorium, Dr. Marjorie Darkland, all smiles, visited him daily and gave him two pills—one red and one green. After Ritchie took his pills, the beautiful woman, his wife, would come and visit.

The scenes went by like a flip book and, as days or weeks or whatever he was showing Michaela and Lisette flipped by. Slowly, smiles returned and the twinkling light came back to both Ritchie's and his beloved's eyes.

Then, the flipping froze.

It featured Ritchie's wife with a concerned look, whispering into his ear.

This time, it was Lisette who spoke. "Something is wrong, Ritchie. What happened?"

The next scene showed the Darkland doctors swooping down Ritchie's wife at the door of the sanatorium, just like the guys in turbans had swooped down on Ritchie in Desert Storm.

As the scenes flipped by, it showed the doctors ushering her down into some sort of basement. Dr. Roland held her while Dr. Marjorie stuck a needle in her neck. Then, they both stood back while Ritchie's young, beautiful wife wilted like a spring daisy in the dead of winter. Roland grabbed a shovel and began to dig, while the heartbreaking onslaught of memories kept on playing. As the pages flipped, they followed Marjorie up the stairs and into Ritchie's room.

"Oh no." Michaela hid her face. "Ritchie, please. I don't want to watch this. I can't."

The movie didn't stop. Against her better judgment, Michaela watched through her fingers.

Marjorie took out a bottle filled with green capsules. She took the capsules apart and emptied them into another little plastic cup. Thought bubbles flew out of Ritchie's head as she worked.

Ritchie and his wife, together and happy.

Someday having a family together.

Maybe even getting a (little) dog.

Then, the words *thank you* surrounded his smiling face. *Thank you for making me well.*

Marjorie turned to him with the same gentle smile she'd worn every day and handed him the cup filled with the powder of an entire bottle of the green pills. A thought bubble appeared above Marjorie's head. *Time to go home.*

Ritchie swallowed the contents and returned her beaming smile.

The next scene showed Ritchie in his hospital bed, and an orderly covering his face with his sheet. Marjorie Darkland was there. Another thought bubble appeared by her head. *Suicide.*

Silence filled the little closet until Michaela's curiosity got the best of her. "What was she whispering to you, Ritchie? Your wife, I mean, in the scene before the doctors ..."

Though Ritchie's outline was no longer visible, another scene lit up the mirror in answer.

The scenes played out as a flip book again, and showed Ritchie's wife coming in through another door.

"She was lost," Michaela observed.

She wandered the halls and peeked through a door. Inside, a pair of orderlies held a woman down. One stuck something into her mouth, but whatever it was didn't stifle her scream. The other charged a battery on a rolling cart.

Ritchie's wife turned away, but the woman's screams followed her down the dim corridor. She started to run and turned down a misbegotten hallway. In front of her, Dr. Roland Darkland dragged a woman across the hallway. By her hair.

She froze.

Apparently, the woman wasn't moving fast enough because Dr. Darkland yanked hard. The woman whimpered as a fistful of her bloody scalp and matted hair came off in his hand. Ritchie's wife gasped and ran, but not before Dr. Darkland saw her.

By the time she made it to Ritchie's room, it was too late.

"Is this why you bang the cabinet doors? You hit my dad, you know."

"Those *doctors* stole our wedding rings." Rage seethed from Ritchie. "I want them back."

Ritchie ended the horrific show with a picture of him and his wife. Both were smiling. Michaela stared into the mirror. "Maybe we can help you find them."

Lisette's voice was quiet in the heavy darkness. "Ritchie, do you know what happened to Rochelle? In the master bathroom?"

"Yes."

The picture on the mirror changed back to the image of Dr. Darkland holding the woman by the hair in the hallway. Her eyes were empty and the doctor towered over her, her bloody scalp dripping from his fist.

Tears welled in Michaela's eyes and her stomach felt funny. Then, she threw up.

CHAPTER SIX

LISETTE

Even though Michaela and Lisette had befriended Ritchie, and even though she had walked back to the playroom and scraped up all the salt so Ritchie could go home, Michaela still couldn't sleep. The shadows of the front yard trees danced across her far wall. She was watching them when she realized something odd. It wasn't the ghosts living (or non-living) in her house that bothered her. It was Ritchie's story of what humans did to other helpless humans that haunted her.

Taking care to be quiet, she pulled back her sheet and comforter and kicked her legs out of bed. It was a short walk to her closet and, despite it being so dark, she strode right in. Luckily, she had cleaned up the vomit and done quite a good job. She couldn't even smell that she'd been sick in there.

A story that her mother had told her once popped into her mind. "I never had to clean up after myself when I vomited when I lived at home. Mom or Dad took care of it for me. But when I got my own place, that all changed. The first time I caught the stomach virus and had to clean up after myself, I realized exactly what adulthood was all about. I didn't want to be grown up anymore."

Michaela felt a kinship with her mom through that story. After tonight, she understood exactly what she was talking about. *I feel more grown up than a ninety-nine-year-old after Ritchie's story.*

"Lisette? Are you here?"

"Yes."

"I couldn't sleep."

"I never sleep." Lisette was clicking something in the back of the closet. "I never had a best friend before, Michaela. But you're the best friend I ever had, so I would like to tell you something."

Michaela leaned forward and peered into her closet mirror. Lisette only appeared places other than the mirror sometimes, and today wasn't one of those times. From the reflection over her shoulder, she watched her friend's thick black braids glisten and move in the dim light, no doubt as they had in life. "You're my best friend too, Lisette. My *meilleur ami.*"

Lisette smiled a sweet, innocent smile. Michaela returned it.

"You asked me once how I became a ghost. I want to share my story with you."

Michaela nodded. "What happened, Lisette?"

The mirror images of the friends melted away, like hot butter in a skillet. In its place formed a fuzzy scene from years gone by. Michaela watched as the people came into focus. They were fussing around an 1800's style buckboard. The horses stomped, a dog barked, and a beautiful young couple climbed onto the seat. Lisette's voice was all around though Michaela could no longer see her.

"My parents said we had to go into town in the buckboard. We needed nails and a wheel and … I don't remember what else. But if I had known what white sugar tasted like then, I would have begged them for some of that, too."

Lisette's voice grew far away as the scene before her animated and captivated all of Michaela's senses.

"Lisette," the woman called through her bright smile. Her voice was thick with a French accent. "Climb up, we must go now."

The heat was stifling, almost unbearable, until a rogue breeze rustled the tall prairie grass and sent the scent of soft lemon over them. Scenic Mountain stood tall and proud nearby. Michaela sensed it was somehow younger and more innocent than it was today, as though it had yet to be filled with the filthy secrets it so wanted to purge.

"Please *Mamah*, let me stay here with Dog." Lisette stood in the prairie grasses. Her hair was black as onyx and glistened just as much. The hem of her handmade gingham dress fell just below her knees, as though she'd outgrown it long ago. Still, her bright smile mirrored her mother's.

A fat German shepherd pup bounced about at her feet and flattened the grass. Grasshoppers scattered.

It's Dog!

Lisette dropped her hand to Dog's head and he licked her wildly. "Please? He will be lonesome for me if I go."

Her father spoke from the driver's seat. "Come now Lisette. It gets hotter still. We will go and be back before your silly pup knows you are gone." He pointed to the house with the stiff end of one of the reins. "He will sleep in the shade there. Your papa knows. Now come."

The horses stomped, obviously eager to be on their way. And no doubt just as eager to discover what breeze could be found on the trail to town.

Lisette looked from her parents down to her dog, who now sat cock-eared at her feet, and hesitated. "But—

Her father's musical voice was more stern than before. "Come now Lisette. Dog will be fine. And you know I have already killed seven rattlesnakes just this week. If you were to get bitten with nobody here—"

Her mother's hand fell on his knee, effectively shushing him. "Please Gerard. Do not speak of such things."

Gerard's grim face softened. "*Oui*, Aimee."

Defeat colored her face as Lisette strode to the buckboard and climbed in the back. Dog yipped and jumped, one ear straight up and the other bent down in the middle, as Gerard popped the reins.

"Yah!" With a lurch, the little family was on their way to town.

Not keen to be left behind, Dog started after them, but stopped short and looked at the ground.

Lisette perked, her coffee-brown eyes wide with worry. Her lips moved but made no sound. Michaela read the word easily.

Snake.

Lisette dared a peek over her shoulder at her parents, who sat straight-backed on the driver's bench. Ever silent, she slipped off the back of the rickety wagon and dropped low into the tall, waving grass. She stared at the wagon as it rounded the side of Scenic Mountain and disappeared over a small rise. Finally, she rose from her hiding spot and dusted off her dress. Her full lips spread into a wide grin as she whirled around and lit out for her home, and for her dog.

Michaela watched as Lisette's focus shifted from the fuzzy brown body of the pup to his obscured head. The big-footed pup gnawed ruthlessly on a ratty ball.

"Not a snake," Lisette said. Her musical words made the pup sit up and take notice of her. He barked a sharp greeting before turning his attentions back to the ball. "Here, Dog. Let me throw it for you."

Lisette bent over and plucked up the soggy ball. Dog yipped as Lisette gave it a hurl. A silver stream of spittle trailed it until it landed with a soppy bounce behind a spiny bunch of cactus. Dog was a streak of brown and black, parting the tall grass like Moses parted the Red Sea. He appeared at Lisette's feet a moment later, the ball dripping from between his teeth. He plopped his rump on the ground and his tail broomed up the dirt in thick puffs.

"Again, *mon ami?*" Lisette pulled the ball from Dog's mouth and flung it as hard as she could. It bounced off a cluster of rocks on the far side of the yard and rolled under a small ledge. A flash of worry contorted Lisette's doll-like features.

Papa said don't go there.

Lisette must have thought the words, but Michaela heard them.

Dog was off like a shot from a pistol, cutting through the grass with his sights set on his slobbery prize.

"Dog, no! Come!" Lisette started after him, but her dress kept catching on hidden arms of mesquite that reached from the ground. "Do not go there! Snakes!"

The hem of her dress ripped free of the devil thorns just as her toe met a rock. Lisette fell hard. Her hand landed in a cactus and the gritty dirt rubbed her knees like sandpaper. Her breath left her lungs in a huff and she bit her tongue. She spat a mouthful of blood and looked up as Dog breached the ledge and disappeared beneath it. Tears hung in her fringe of lashes and her lower lip began to tremble. From where she sat, Michaela could tell they weren't tears born of pain.

Lisette pushed herself to her feet. Blood streamed down

her legs and into her scuffed shoes. Tears streaked her cheeks like wet ribbons as she ran for Dog. The horrific sound met her ears at once.

A tell-tale rattle buzzed to life in the darkness of the rocky cave. Then another, then another, then another. Michaela somehow heard Lisette's urgent thought.

It's a den.

Dog barked a chorus of shrill and surprised barks. The hideous rattles that promised death sang out of the den like a choir of bloodthirsty hangmen—and dawn was fast approaching.

"Come here Dog!" The words tore from Lisette's throat in a hysterical scream, but it was too late.

Dog yelped once, then twice. Lisette lost count as she dropped to her knees in front of the deadly den. The yelps melded into a sickening, terrified cry. A cry for help from her only friend. Without thinking too far into the future, Lisette reached into the den.

Her fingers closed around Dog's scruffy neck in an instant. "Come on," she cried. Her words were too high pitched to be her own. She pulled hard, but Dog was dead weight. She pulled harder and something hit her arm. Lisette ignored it and kept pulling. Something hit her other arm, right between the fingers. Dog let go a quiet, helpless whine.

Finally, she managed to heft Dog into the sunlight. His little body was already puffy and swollen, especially his paws and his shiny black nose. From his back leg hung a young rattler who hadn't let go. Lisette grabbed and yanked, effectively breaking the needlelike fangs off in Dog's flesh. Dog lay still, with only the quietest whine in his swollen throat.

"It's all right, Dog," Lisette cooed. She pulled her dying

friend into her lap. "*Mamah* and *Papa* will be home soon. They will help us ... they will ..." It wasn't until then that she saw her own hand and arm, swelling and discoloring as she looked on in terror.

Lisette tilted her body sideways and her eyes rolled back into her skull, but her arms held on to the dog whose breathing was coming in sharp, quick gasps, until she was on her side and curled around dying Dog.

The world turned to waves and her head felt heavy. "It will be all right, Dog," she whispered. Her voice sounded strangled. "As soon as *Mamah* and *Papa* return. They will ... make us ... better ..."

Dog's rapid breathing stopped as Lisette laid her head on his lifeless body.

The movie-like scenes faded from the mirror and left Michaela staring at her own reflection in the dark closet. Her mouth hung agape.

Lisette's visage didn't appear over Michaela's shoulder as it had so many times before, but her voice was clear in the dark closet. "I hope *Mamah* and *Papa* find their way home soon. I'm growing so much tired of waiting. And I miss them."

Michaela found her voice. "Why can't I see you?"

Lisette's voice was a fuzzy echo in the tiny room. "I do not want my friend to see me cry."

Rochelle

Tim was right. He said before that he was certain the wind whipped down Scenic Mountain, right into the house. And it did.

Addie tossed and turned as the faint howl outside her window whistled through the trees. Beside her and beneath a nest of blankets, Tim groaned. The bathroom light was on again as she lay there thinking about her latest rejection letter for *A Heart on Hold*. The form letter from a publishing house had at least been personalized this time.

```
Dear Ms. Smithfield,
With   such   a   variety   Christian
themes  (such  as  faith,  monogamy,
and  prayer)  that  ran  through  the
manuscript  and  no  doubt  inspired
the  author  to  query  us,  we  can't
help  but  wonder  why  the  author  felt
the  need  to  add  such  bloody  and
horrific  battle  scenes  to  her  manu-
script.  Our  readers  are  looking  for
an  HEA,  (happily  ever  after),  which
the  author  provided,  but  they  don't
want  to  walk  such  a  bloody  road  to
```

```
get there.  Cut the battle scenes
and reconsider the lineage of the
young mulatto slave named Cotton,
then requery us.
Sincerely,
Omnibus Publishing—2018's Top Ten
Publishers in Texas
```

Why did they refer to me in third person? Like they thought someone else would be reading my email?

The bathroom light flicked off as Adelaide stared at the wall and wondered if she should put 'aspiring author' on her resume or just leave it off and start the job hunt Monday. She flopped onto her side and elicited another groan from her husband.

It's no use. I may as well get up before I wake Tim.

From the corner of her eye, the bathroom light flicked on again. Addie shut her eyes tight, but they sprang open on their own.

Seriously. It's a short. Time to put this matter to rest once and for all.

She pushed the memory of the hideous creature in the pink and blue bathroom out of her mind and stepped into the dressing area.

I refuse to be scared of my imagination, especially in my own house. This is the product of too many late nights and too much coffee.

Addie peeked inside the bathroom. Nothing was there. She exhaled the breath she didn't know she was holding.

If my former students could see me being so scared, they would help Tim cart me off to the loony bin.

She reached up to shut off the light. When her fingers touched the switch, it happened.

A deafening buzz, like the sound produced when they charged the old fashioned electric chair, sounded all around her and filled her ears. The light brightened so that she had to squint.

Feels like I'm in surgery, but I'm not asleep.

Addie tried to yank her hand away from the switch, but she couldn't.

I'm being electrocuted by that faulty wire.

Before her, the creature appeared again.

Rochelle.

They stared at one another, neither speaking. Even if they did, nothing could be heard over the incessant buzzing. Addie couldn't help but stare at the creature that had materialized before her. She was even more hideous than before, with blood oozing from her scalp. Her lips were twisted into a permanent scowl and her eyes, oh those eyes. Black, sad holes.

I wonder what she sees when she looks at me?

"Come on Rochelle," a phantom voice said. "Let's go out tonight." The voice echoed as though the words were spoken through a long, metal pipe.

A surge of excitement made Addie's heart pound faster as a conversation she never had played out in her head as she stared into Rochelle's lifeless eyes.

In Addie's mind, she was looking into the mirror. Except, Addie's reflection didn't stare back at her. Instead, what she saw was a beautiful young woman with long black hair that shimmered like gossamer on her shoulders, and her bright, round green eyes. She picked up some sparkly perfume and spritzed it on her front, making her sparkle. "Okay!"

Oh my, this is Rochelle I'm looking at!

"How long have you been up?" the phantom voice asked in its reverberating tones.

Rochelle held up three fingers to the mirror and giggled. Apparently, the phantom voice was somewhere behind her.

"Three days! Are you *sure* you aren't on something?"

Rochelle balked in the mirror, her big eyes even wider with feigned disdain. "Drugs? Really? No way—you know me better than that. I don't even like taking Tylenol."

"Then how are you still up?"

The sparkle came back to Rochelle's emerald eyes. "I don't know. Sometimes, life just feels so very beautiful. Like it would be a sin to sleep and miss even one second of it." She shrugged. "I don't expect you to understand—I don't even get it. But anyway, come on. The night is young and so are we!"

Giggles faded as Rochelle skipped out of the room and slammed the door behind her. Addie was left staring into a dark mirror, apparently in Rochelle's bathroom. A moment later, the giggling returned. This time, it was louder and much more animated and punctuated with something Addie couldn't quite discern.

She stared into the mirror as the front door burst open and Rochelle stumbled in. Right behind her, with his hands on her waist, stumbled a young man with hair as black as night and a leather jacket covering a white undershirt. A cigarette was tucked over his ear, but he didn't seem to want to smoke. At least not yet.

His lips found Rochelle's neck as she pushed his jacket off his shoulders. It fell in a heap on the floor.

"What was your name again," she asked in breathless gasps.

The boy relieved her of her white tank top. "Does it matter, Roseanne?"

Her name is Rochelle, Adelaide thought brusquely.

He pushed her back onto her messy, unmade bed. "From the way you came onto me at the club, I didn't think you were the kind of girl who did much talking."

Rochelle's giggles fizzled into a white screen as the nameless boy climbed on top of her.

Addie struggled to force a thought into her mind. *Rochelle, if you can hear me, why are you showing me this?"*

Rochelle's bathroom mirrors disappeared, and the real world was in front of her eyes again. Well, the real world and a decrepit phantom with a story to tell.

There wasn't a glimmer of the beautiful young girl in the hideous beast before her. She'd somehow been reduced to a skeletal shell of a human. A *dead* human.

"I'm so scared," the fearsome Rochelle said. The voice was different than the beautiful, young Rochelle in the memories. Raspy. Hollow. Haunted. "I'm cold, it's so tiny in here, and I'm so scared. Help me, Adelaide."

Still, Addie couldn't move her hand from the buzzing light switch. The thought that she was having a psychotic break flashed briefly in her mind.

Okay, Adelaide thought. *Okay Rochelle. Show me how to help you.*

The bathroom mirror appeared again and rays of sun splayed across Rochelle's bed that was still shared by the young man. A sudden banging on the door made him jump. Rochelle didn't move.

Swearing under his breath, he didn't look at Rochelle as he swung his legs over the side of the bed. He stood up and pulled on his pants before he stomped to the door and flung it open. "Yeah, what do you want?"

A woman in a muumuu stood like a wall in front of the door. "I'm the landlord and I want my rent. It's two weeks overdue," she yelled.

He laughed at the overweight grandma with pink foam curlers in her hair.

"I don't know what you think you're laughing at, Sonny. That girl in there is crazy. Plain ape crazy!"

"Keep your shirt on, Grandma. She'll pay you when she can."

Slam.

"Rosie, wake up. Your landlord's mad, babe. She's gonna call the cops if you don't pay up." The nameless boy shook her shoulder. "Rosie?"

"My name is Rochelle," Rochelle groaned. "Leave me alone."

He pulled his shirt on and picked up his jacket. "Aw, baby. After all we meant to each other?"

Rochelle pulled the blanket over her head. "Close the window."

He picked up her purse and rummaged through. Addie saw him look at her driver's license. "Rochelle, yeah. So it is." He put it back but pulled out a twenty and stuck it in his pocket. "Ah, it's for the best anyway. I could never explain you to my wife."

The scene fizzled but was immediately replaced by an older man standing over Rochelle's bed.

"Get up Rochelle," he demanded. "You've been laying here for weeks. Get up."

"Close the windows, Dad," she gurgled. Her voice sounded desperate and exhausted at the same time.

A woman's voice spoke, high and shrill, in the background. Addie tried to see who was speaking, but she couldn't.

"Yes, Big Spring Sanatorium?" the woman said loudly. "I need to admit my daughter."

Still, Rochelle's dad danced around her bed, desperate for an idea to help his baby girl. It appeared as though his race was run.

"Huh? No, I don't know what's wrong with her. She's crazy!" The woman screeched into the phone. Addie wondered if she looked like the fat woman in the muumuu. "What do I mean by crazy? I mean she stays up for days and goes out with men and runs wild. Then, something in her hits a switch and she won't get out bed for weeks. Begs to be left alone in the dark. If that's not crazy I don't know what is. How do you treat something so crazy anyway?"

Rochelle's dad pushed a pile of clothes off a chair in the corner and sunk into it. His head hung low and his shoulders shook. When he sniffled and batted at his face, Addie knew he was crying.

"Electro-shock therapy and medication? I guess it sounds okay, but I don't know nothin' about nothin'. Y'all are the experts on that stuff." Her mother slammed down a phone. Papers rustled in the background. "They're coming to get her, George. Then she won't be our problem anymore."

The scene faded, but an image burst into her mind like a shooting star across a black sky. A group of people, all dressed in black, were huddled around a tombstone. The image zoomed in on the epitaph. It simply read, 'Dad,' before the image fizzled as quickly as it had come.

Again, Addie's vision transformed back into the present. At last, she seemed to be unfrozen.

"Oh Rochelle," Addie said. "You were bipolar."

The phrase the nurse had used during her miscarriage popped into Addie's mind without warning.

God's will.

She pushed it away and focused on the flickering image before her instead. Poor Rochelle. Everything about her short, tragic life was wrong. "Then your mother had you committed, against your father's wishes. But he died, didn't he."

Rochelle's visage had taken on a morose air as Addie unraveled her entire life's story in just a few short scenes. "I wish there was something I could do to make this better for you," Addie thought hard. "When you needed someone, nobody was there."

Rochelle was silent.

Adelaide thought briefly about returning to bed and seeing if she could fall asleep. *Maybe it was Rochelle's angst that was keeping me awake this whole time.*

She changed her mind at once.

"How could you dare be so selfish, Addie? Thinking of your sleep at a time like this."

She spoke aloud to the ghost who flickered before her, staring at her, waiting for something, but it seemed neither of them knew what that something was. "If I can ever help you, please just tell me what to do. Okay?"

Rochelle turned her head and peered at Addie through lifeless eyes. The harmonic voice filled the bathroom and bounced off the pink and blue tiles like a ping pong ball. "Please leave the light on in here. I'm so terribly afraid of the dark."

"I can do better than that. I'll be right back."

Addie trotted into the bedroom and rummaged in her

top dresser drawer. Her hand closed around the roll of duct tape almost instantly.

"Addie?" Tim's voice was heavy with sleep. "What in the world are you doing?"

Should I tell him? He may commit me to Crestview.

She tore off a strip of the silver cure-all before disappearing into the bathroom. "I'm fixing the light in here."

True to her work and her word, Addie taped the light switch in the *on* position. "There Miss Rochelle. It's not going anywhere, at least not easily." She smiled at the gruesome phantom. "Everyone is scared of something. I'm scared of small spaces, myself."

"I know," Rochelle responded in the lifeless voice that seemed to be filtered through time and space before it reached Addie's ears. "I pulled you out when you got stuck in the hamper. I couldn't let you be scared. Nobody should ever have to be scared."

CHAPTER EIGHT

THE DARKLAND DOCTORS

Michaela awoke to discover Lisette's face positioned inches from hers. Her sleepy eyes widened and her breath caught in her throat. She coughed. No matter how much she liked Lisette, her dark, eyeless sockets were spooky even when she was expecting her. When she wasn't expecting her, the young, French ghost's visage was downright terrifying.

Still, Lisette stared at her. *Through* her.

"Good morning, *mon ami*," Michaela managed. Her heart hammered in her chest.

"Today's the day," Lisette warned. "Be ready."

Michaela pushed herself up in the bed. The black, fuzzy headboard with large faux diamonds knocked against the wall. Something knocked back.

Probably Ritchie.

She stretched, rubbed her eyes, and yawned twice.

"Does it always take you this long to wake up?" Lisette's impatience colored her normally musical words. "We have much to do."

Michaela flung back her comforter with the kitty cats on it. "Well, I'm hungry. So, can whatever we have to do wait until I get something to eat for breakfast?"

"*Oui.* I suppose so."

"Do you ever get hungry?"

"No."

Michaela pulled a red fluffy robe on over her night clothes. "My parents keep asking me what happened to the sugar. Did I leave it in here?"

Lisette grinned. "Yes."

"Is there any left?"

She shook her ghostly head. "No."

Michaela yawned again and stifled a giggle as she padded to her closed bedroom door. "Okay, I will be back in a minute." She turned the knob but paused and turned back to face her friend. "Lisette? What *is* happening today that has you all worked up?"

"The Darkland doctors are coming."

Michaela's jaw dropped so quickly it popped. Without a word, she walked out of her room and opened the hidden purple door that led to the front yard. After surveying the outside world from behind the safety of the glass storm door, she stepped into the front yard.

She'd slept in. The sun, straight overhead, was a pale disc behind an overcast sky. Thick black clouds loomed low on the horizon. A cold wind swirled through the late summer grass and brought goosebumps to Michaela's arms and legs.

Dad calls that a North Wind.

She narrowed her eyes. Something in her park-like yard felt off. Instead of feeling safe and secure, Michaela was aware of something entirely different. The birds hopped from branch to branch—but didn't sing. Squirrels didn't dash and chase and chatter. Instead, they sat up on their fluffy haunches and stared. She glanced over her shoulder at the looming Scenic Mountain. If by some chance it had eyes, she knew they would be staring straight at her.

"It's like everything is waiting for something. Anticipating it." Her voice even sounded off.

A slick black Cadillac DeVille slinked around the corner and drove slowly up the block.

Like a snake stalking a mouse.

Michaela ducked behind a prickly pear and watched as it cruised by. The windows were tinted to the point of blackness and she couldn't see inside. Still, she knew who was inside.

"It's them." Her voice was a whisper. "The evil doctors have come home."

When the car rounded the far corner, Michaela ran back into the house but paused long enough to carefully double check that her secret entrance was truly locked behind her.

Lisette's voice was a hiss as she passed her room. "They're coming, *mon ami.* They're close."

Michaela didn't stop to chat. Instead, she ran down the long hall. "Mom? Dad?"

Nope, nobody's in the bathroom where Mom likes to shower.

Something banged hard when she turned her back and ran back down the hall.

Bang, bang, bang!

It sounded like a toddler who discovered that once you open a cabinet, they're fun to slam. The harder and louder the better.

Bang, bang, bang!

Michaela stopped and looked back into the dim bathroom. Something that felt a little like icy fear dripped down her back. She swallowed hard. "Ritchie, it's okay."

Bang!

"I'm going to find your wedding rings. Don't be mad."

Bang!

An odd sensation brought a rash of tingles to her skin.

Is it really going to be okay? Are you really the person who can promise that and keep that promise in the end?

Michaela's throat tightened and she forced a swallow. "I promise to try my best."

She waited, but nothing slammed.

"Michaela, stop slamming doors, please." Her mother's voice echoed from another part of the house.

Remembering her mission, Michaela took off down the hall toward the sound of Addie's voice. She raced against a clock she couldn't see, for people who were no longer real. *But they're real to me.*

"Mom?" Michaela slowed when she caught sight of the trees through the front window. They whipped wild, back and forth, back and forth, as they danced the dance of the summer thunderstorms. Black clouds painted a sinister backdrop and the wind that whipped the trees whistled down through the rock fireplace. A bright flash made her cover her eyes. The storm was here.

"Mom!"

A deafening crack of thunder drown out any response. A hand fell on her shoulder. Michaela screamed.

"Hush baby, it's me. It's Mom, you're all right. Just a storm, see?" Gently, she moved Michaela's hands from over her eyes.

More flashes lit the world outside. They were so close, she could hear the sizzling zips that came with each lightning strike.

"We're right in the middle of the it, but we're safe in here."

"This house is built for storms, isn't it Mom?" Michaela's throat hurt from her jagged screech. "I mean, it's going to be okay, right?"

"Yes it is. Whoever designed this place really did a good job."

"I bet my blanket fort is halfway down the block by now." Michaela bit her tongue. "Where's Dad?"

Addie looked thoughtful. "He's here somewhere, I'm not sure what project he was planning to start."

"Here." Addie clasped her hands on Michaela's shoulders and guided her toward the kitchen. "Did you find your surprise I left you the other day? The chewy cinnamon candy you love? You never mentioned it."

"No—" *Lisette. Did she take my candy?*

Bam!

The glass in the sparkly dining room rattled. Michaela and Addie jumped.

"Um, that wasn't thunder." Michaela's voice wavered. "Thunder doesn't hit the window." She stared at her mother, begging with her eyes for her to make everything all right. "What was that?"

Addie stared at the glass. "You're right. Something hit the window." She started toward the door. A chilled breeze swept past them. "But I have no idea what it could have been."

She took a step toward the windows. "Tim? Honey?"

Michaela grasped her hands at her middle and watched her mother walk slowly across the dining room toward the noise. She opened the back door and at once, the sounds of the storm intensified.

It sounds angry.

Addie gasped.

"What is it Mom?"

Addie stepped out the back door and into the swirling wind. A few drops of rain speckled the windows and the patio as though someone had thrown handfuls of water hither and yon. "Oh my goodness ... it's a—"

Michaela took a couple of steps toward the back door. "It's a what?"

"Where did it—" Addie's voice trailed off as she crouched low. Michaela crept up to the window and studied her mom's hunched figure. She looked to be creeping up on something.

"Oh my—Michaela—help!"

Michaela dashed out the back door. A handful of icy raindrops hit her in the face. Addie fell backwards, her arms flung over her head. "Stop it, go away!"

She kicked wildly with her bare feet. "Go away!"

The mess of beating wings and feathers were drowned out by Addie's shrieks.

Michaela skidded to a halt. Her mouth fell open when the animal's yellow eyes fixed on her. "It's an owl!"

With wings spread wide, the creature of the night took flight and disappeared over the house, all the while not taking its eyes off Michaela. The way its head turned to keep eye contact as it glided over the roof promised to haunt her nightmares when she least expected it. Addie's soft sobs broke her reverie.

Michaela snapped to attention and dashed to her mother's side. "Mom, are you okay?"

Spots of blood had already soaked into the sandstone patio rocks. More still streamed down her mother's face. Michaela grabbed Addie's trembling hands and pulled them down in an effort to survey the damage. "Here, let's get you inside."

Addie managed to get to her feet with Michaela's help. "Is it, is it bad?"

Michaela couldn't make eye contact with her mother.

Addie would see right through her to the answers Michaela didn't want to give. Just like she always did. "Looks like it got your forehead a bit."

When they stepped into the house, a torrential sheet of rain and hail peppered the roof and blotted out the view from the windows that had moments before been clear. It was as though a thick white cloud descended on them. It echoed through the house like an onslaught of Vikings against the last medieval fortress in England. They were trapped in their castle. Helpless. Hopeless. With no other choice than to wait out the siege and hope they didn't take too bad of a beating.

The doorbell rang as Michaela helped Addie into the front bathroom with the 1950's up-and-down lights. Tim's chipper voice rose above the storm noise. She peeked out the stained-glass window while Addie washed her face.

Through the torrents of rain, she could just make out the black DeVille in their driveway.

"Oh no," Michaela squeaked. "The Vikings have breached the wall."

Her dad laughed his welcoming, rollicking laugh. "Drs. Roland and Marjorie Darkland, what a surprise! We've heard so much about you, what a pleasure to have you in our—well, in *your*—home. Come on in."

"Thankfully, the lacerations from the owl's talons aren't deep enough to warrant stitches," Addie managed. "But the puncture wounds poked pretty far into my scalp."

"Here Mom," Michaela pressed a cold, wet rag to the longest bloody scratch. "Hold this here." Michaela noticed that her mother's hands finally quit shaking as she held the rag to her forehead. "It goes across your forehead, the big one does, and into your hairline. But it isn't that deep at all."

"Thank heaven for small favors," Addie quipped. Her voice zinged a bit like she might laugh ... or cry. "Do we have any of that clear bandage glue? Do you know?"

"I haven't seen any, Mom."

"Was it going for my eyes," Addie wondered aloud as Michaela peeled the rag away from her head.

"Hey, it quit bleeding already. Cool." She patted Addie on the shoulder. "Good job with your clotting skills, Mom."

Michaela dropped to her knees as Addie sank down on top of the toilet and leaned against the wall. She rummaged under the sink for a moment until she found what she was looking for.

"I'll go ahead and tell you I'm sorry before I do this," Michaela said, hiding the rubbing alcohol behind her back. "If it burns, pretend Dad poured it. Okay?"

Adelaide laughed a tired laugh. "Deal. Pour some *alcohol* on me," she sang. "I would have said sugar, but the sugar seems to have sprouted little legs and walked away."

Michaela smacked the cold rag over her mother's face. "Hold this here so it doesn't get in your eyes."

"Ow."

Michaela held the bottle at ready. "One ... two ..." She tilted it and watched through squinted eyes as the clear liquid rained down over her mother's wounds.

"Okay," Addie said when Michaela finally quit pouring. "*That* was like liquid fire."

"You didn't even squeal," Mack said. "I'm impressed."

Addie dabbed at the wayward streams of alcohol that continued to run down her face. "That was so strange, I've never heard of an owl attack on a human before."

"Me neither." Michaela put the lid back on the empty

bottle of alcohol and tossed it into the basket. She looked at her mother, but hesitated. "Mom?"

Addie tore off a square of toilet paper and swiped at her hairline. "Yeah?"

"Dad said the Darkland doctors were here." Michaela dropped her voice. "I don't like them, Mom."

Addie stopped dabbing. "You don't even know them."

Michaela set her jaw. "You always told me to listen to my gut, Mom. And my gut says no to the Darkland docs."

Addie's lips tilted into a half smile. "The Darkland docs, huh. That sounds like a rather notorious name." As she stood, something flashed in her mother's eyes, but Michaela couldn't quite be sure what it was. Anyway, it was gone as quickly as it was noticed. "Come on, let's get out there."

I have to stall.

Michaela plopped down on the toilet lid. "I can't go out there. I have diabetic nerve pain in my feet."

Addie looked like someone let the air out of her, the way she slumped in the shoulders. "Honey, we have been through this. You cannot physically have diabetic nerve pain."

"Oh, but I can. And I do."

Her mother closed her eyes and appeared to be taking great care in keeping her voice even. "In order to have diabetic nerve pain, you have to first have diabetes. You, Michaela, do not have diabetes."

"How do you know?" *If I stall long enough, maybe the doctors will leave.* "You can't be sure that I am not diabetic, Mom."

Adelaide turned her back to her daughter and placed her hand on the bathroom doorknob. "Sweetie, the last time you informed me you had diabetic nerve pain, I bought you a glucometer. Remember? The kit with the little needle that pricks your finger with the little machine that then tests your blood sugar?"

Michaela nodded. "Of course I remember. That little needle hurt."

Addie turned to face her. Her cheeks had grown scarlet over the course of their conversation, and Michaela didn't think it had anything to do with the alcohol or owl. She wasn't smiling.

"All right. I'll make you a deal. I will prove to you that you do not have diabetic nerve pain. When I do, you have to follow me out into our home to greet the people who, for whatever reason, came to visit us. Deal?"

Addie stuck out her hand.

Michaela cupped her chin and propped one leg up on the opposite knee.

"Michaela." Addie's voice was deadpan serious.

"Fine." She shook her mother's hand.

"Good," Addie said. "Now, let me find that glucometer."

Michaela tucked her fingertips into her fist and hopped to her feet. "Guess what, Mom."

"I bet I can guess," Addie said. Her words dripped in pseudo-excitement. "I bet your diabetic nerve pain is miraculously cured."

"Give the lady a prize," Michaela said through a tight smile. "Let's go."

Michaela trudged out of the bathroom behind her mother. Soft talking directed them to the big living room with the rock fireplace.

"Honey," Tim said, rising from the couch. "I'd like you to meet Drs. Roland and Marjorie Darkland." He put his arm around her waist and guided her next to him. "Drs., this is my wife, Adelaide. This young lady here is our beautiful daughter, Michaela."

Addie extended her hand and offered a warm smile. "Doctors," she said. "What a pleasant surprise." She gestured to the picture windows that sat on either side of the natural rock fireplace. "And it looks like you made it here just in time. This storm is an ugly one."

Michaela didn't speak. Instead, she skulked around the back of the couch and slid down into the recliner at the far end of the room. She pulled her knees up to her chest and surveyed the visitors.

Marjorie clasped a black medical bag in one hand and returned Addie's smile.

I wonder if all women doctors have purses that look like old time medical bags. Is it, like, a fashion statement at the Retired Doctors Club?

"Oh, you don't have to worry dear," she said. Her words had some sort of soft accent. Irish maybe? "This house is built strong. Will stand up to any storm Texas throws at it."

Wrinkles fanned out from the old woman's eyes when she smiled, giving her a warm and grandmotherly appearance. Her gray hair, meticulously curled and sprayed, sat like a poof on her head. And her bifocal glasses with the coke bottle lenses were yellowed with age. She was about a head shorter than her husband, who stood at her side.

Clad in all black, Roland Darkland neither smiled nor looked particularly friendly. In fact, he looked like a man who had just stepped out of a funeral parlor and wanted to be anywhere but here. His narrow eyes darted around, like a rabbit watching for the fox. His back was ever so slightly hunched, but he still stood a solid six feet in height.

As everyone sat back down, Michaela noticed that he had a black medical bag, too. However, his was peeking out from behind the loveseat where he and Marjorie sat.

Maybe they get more points for matching. Michaela bit back a smile. *And double points if the man is gutsy enough to carry a man-purse at all.*

Icy fingers of fear clawed at her gut despite the brief moment of jocularity.

"Well now," Addie began. She crossed her legs. "So tell us. What is it that brings you guys out this way? Didn't the Realtor say you'd retired to an island community somewhere?"

Marjorie leaned forward, her back still achingly straight. "Oh, yes dear. We did."

"Jamaica," Roland added. His voice echoed off the stone floor and brick fireplace.

He sounds like a funeral man, too.

"Left this jewel of a home to our children. We have three you know." She looked lovingly at Roland. "Two doctors and a lawyer, they are."

Roland was somber. "Do you just have the one girl?"

Addie kept her face stoic. "Yes, yes we do. Just our beautiful daughter." She took Tim's hand in hers. "She's all we needed, wasn't she Tim dear?"

Tim shifted in his seat.

Roland glanced at his wife and they shared a raised-eyebrow look. His voice rumbled low, like thunder. "She's simple, isn't she?"

Addie's jaw went slack and her words came in a stammer. "Autistic doesn't mean simple."

Michaela shuddered at the ice in her mother's frosty words.

The old woman cocked her head condescendingly and

spoke through tight lips. "We dealt with plenty of her kind when we ran Big Springs Sanatorium."

"We did," Roland agreed.

Marjorie let go a phony laugh. Michaela chewed her lip.

I will never understand the ways of adults.

"Anyway," Marjorie continued, "our wishes were that the children have this house demolished. But, as you can see, they didn't follow directions very well." She shrugged and forced a painted-on smile. "Kids."

Addie cocked her head. "Demolished? Why ever for?"

"To donate the land to the Scenic Mountain state park across the street," Roland and Marjorie said in unison.

Wow, that was rehearsed.

"I, um, see." Addie fought to keep her lips tilted upward. She turned to Tim with a look in her eye that clearly said *help*.

Tim grinned. "I wish we could retire to Jamaica," he said. "I heard something about success in drug research that helped buy you guys your island time?"

Roland fidgeted. "Boy, news really travels around a small town, doesn't it?"

A boom of thunder went off like a gunshot. Everyone jumped. Everyone except their guests. Down the street, someone's car alarm went off.

"Are you interested in pharmaceuticals?" Roland asked. His bushy eyebrows lay like dead caterpillars, white with age, across the tops of his eyes.

Tim shrugged and nodded.

"Well," Roland began, "we spearheaded a new drug therapy for clinically insane patients at Big Spring Sanatorium."

"It's set to be demolished," Marjorie added. "Any day now."

Roland ignored his wife. "Discovered a new drug all

together, along with the therapy regimen and dosage levels. We have helped many *wonderful* people lead a much better quality of life."

A series of lightning bolts flashed outside the window squelched the conversation. Another boom of thunder followed by an eye-burning flash drove Michaela to duck and cover out of sheer self-preservation. When she dared to lift her head, the world was dark.

Power's out.

She froze.

With an unexpected zap, the lights sputtered back to life. Both Darkland doctors were no longer seated, but instead, stood in the middle of the living room. They clutched their medical bags and looked about ready to jump out of their respective skins. Michaela's pulse sped up as she watched her dad play off the weirdness.

"Wow." Tim jumped to his feet and stood next to Roland. "I do believe that was a direct hit."

Roland nodded. "The old radio tower out back, no doubt." Slowly, the odd doctors sank back onto the loveseat.

A crash sounded from the direction of her parent's bedroom. Addie pushed herself up. Her fake smile was noticeably absent. Michaela could tell that her mother was uneasy. She was uneasy, too. Something about this couple just wasn't right. "I'll check that out, excuse me."

Addie strode purposefully across the living room and disappeared into the hall that led to the master bedroom.

The problematic light flickered from the bathroom when Addie walked into her room. She glanced around, but nothing appeared to be out of place, broken, or knocked over.

"Ad-d-d-d-ie ..."

She recognized Rochelle's voice at once.

"Rochelle!" She stepped into the bathroom.

Sure enough, Rochelle's miserable visage was there. Sadness filled the room, sadness tinged with a hint of frustration. Addie looked at the light switch, which was still taped to Kingdom Come. "You're upset," Addie surmised.

Rochelle reached out a bony hand toward her. Against every natural emotion in her body, Addie took it in her own. "Would you like to tell me more, Rochelle?"

The images, same as the night before, returned and hit Addie like a Mack truck. It felt as though Rochelle was physically shoving her memories into Adelaide's brain. In fact, these images were even *more* vivid than before.

An overwhelming sense of fear was enough to make her want to curl into a ball and hide, right here on the bathroom floor. Anything to make it go away.

An older woman's voice was nasal in her ears. "Rochelle's parents gave us legal guardianship over her."

Adelaide recognized the voice at once. *Marjorie Darkland.*

The memory continued. "I believe she is the perfect candidate for the new course of drug therapy. Let's get her primed. She's manic now, so put her in the light box."

Addie's heart began to pound in sync with Rochelle's as the desperate phantom shared with Addie her memories and experiences, ones which nobody should have had to experience at all.

The light box.

A padded room with no window. Only a constant fluorescent hum lit the room to a bright, unnatural state of eternal glowing. Food was slipped under the door once a day, or at least Rochelle thought it was once a day. Without a way to compare dark and light, there was no sense of time.

After the first tray of food, someone turned on the music. It stayed on through several more trays, loud and thumping. No lyrics, no familiarity, no pausing between tracks. Just the constant state of visual and audible stimulation.

"Nobody ever gave me meds," Rochelle explained. Her voice was higher pitched today. Addie knew the reason behind the sound all too well. Hysteria. "But looking back, I know they were in the water. They were giving me sedatives but keeping me constantly stimulated."

Addie felt Rochelle's agony.

"Once I finally fell asleep," Rochelle continued, "they marked their drug trial a success and took me back to my regular room."

Adelaide began to speak. "Did they at least let you res—"

The memory sequence changed dramatically, and featured Dr. Roland Darkland dragging Rochelle down the hallway by her hair. Still partially sedated, Rochelle didn't move fast enough for the uppity doctor and he yanked her hair. Hard.

Hot bile rose into Addie's throat.

And that piece of human garbage is sitting on my loveseat right now, as though he doesn't have a care in the world.

The image of Roland Darkland hovering above Rochelle, with her once-beautiful locks snarled in his fist, made Addie's stomach threaten to revolt. Pieces of Rochelle's bloody scalp, where she was now bald, dripped droplets of blood onto the white linoleum tile of the hidden hospital wing. On all fours and at the doctor's complete and total mercy, Rochelle whimpered helplessly.

"Oh Rochelle," Addie sniffed. "I don't want to sound

condescending, but you poor baby girl. I wish I could hug you right now."

"Nobody ever wanted to hug me just to hug me," Rochelle said. Addie wondered if she was actually saying the words or thinking them. "Thank you, Addie."

Another image seared itself into Adelaide's brain. Rochelle, restrained in a hospital bed, her mangled head propped awkwardly on a bloody pillow. Someone whisked into the room with a tray of food and left it on the bedside table. Well out of reach of her restrained hands. She felt Rochelle's hunger with every ounce of her being.

What unbelievable torture.

Dr. Darkland himself came in with a bendy-straw and a glass of water. "You did well, Rochelle. Now, you want to help more people like you, right? Sure you do."

He stuck the straw in her mouth. Addie watched her memory as a single tear slid down her cheek. Rochelle was completely helpless, completely alone, and she knew it. She stared up at Roland with hopeful eyes, begging for mercy. Beseeching a bit of human kindness.

Like a dog on death row at the kill shelter.

"Drink this, Rochelle. It will flip the switch in your brain from manic to depressive."

Rochelle did as she was told and drank. And drank. And drank.

Dr. Darkland didn't even bother to feed her a bite of food off the tray. If he had, things may have gone differently.

Addie felt Rochelle's arms turn to stone, followed by her legs. Then, it was hard to breathe.

"Paralyzed," Rochelle explained. "Not even any monitors on me or anything. I was their personal petri dish of experimentation."

When an orderly came to pick up her untouched food tray, he spun on his heel and marched from the room. He found Roland Darkland and reported Rochelle as dead. Her eyelids were heavy and closed, but her mind was sharp as ever.

Dr. Darkland and a team of flunkies rushed in. There was much discussion and checking of charts, but nobody touched her. Nobody checked a pulse, listened to her chest, nothing. *It's like she wasn't even there.* Finally, the conversation in the room ceased and all eyes were on Dr. Roland Darkland. Of course, he had the final say.

"Take her down, boys."

The entire length of the ride through the hall, into the elevator, and down to the basement, Rochelle was screaming. Only nobody could hear her cries.

Like a thoroughbred out of the starting gate, her heart raced faster and faster. As the orderlies talked about their upcoming weekends, her heart sputtered on until it reached inhumane speeds. Tears eked from her eyes and wet her cheeks.

"Look down Man in White, please," Rochelle pleaded silently. "I'm not dead, look at me for God's sake!"

A hysterical madness whirled like a tempest inside her, but her body was of no more use to her than a block of stone.

Man in White slid a long, silver tray out of the wall.

We're in the morgue.

At some point, someone had put her inside of a death shroud. All that was left to do was to be zipped into her eternal cocoon and slid into the wall. Forgotten.

The zipping sound started at her feet and intensified as it grew nearer to her head. Man with the Ugly Mustache did the zipping, but didn't bother to look at her face. He was too busy talking about tonight's high school football game.

By the time it was decided that the home team would annihilate the visiting football team, they turned their attention to her. "This your last one of the day?" Ugly Mustache grasped her ankles.

Man in White grabbed her neck and shoulder, pulling what was left of her hair in the process. Somewhere inside her, she screamed.

"Yup, gotta get this broad on ice, then I'm off for a three-day weekend. And man let me tell you, I'm gonna live these three days."

Ugly Mustache counted down. "Ready on three, two, one. Lift."

They lifted badly and plunked Rochelle down on the morgue tray in tandem. The icy chill of the metal tickled her skin through the thick shroud. Their voices were muffled as someone began to push the tray into the wall.

"Don't. Please, no," Addie and Rochelle thought together. Addie tried to tighten her grip on Rochelle's fingers for support, but they clutched only chilled air. They both knew how this was going to end.

Rochelle's body jerked as one of the men, probably Ugly Mustache, gave the tray the concluding shove. It clanged shut with an eternal finality that she wasn't ready to experience. Adrenaline flooded her veins and the fight or flight instinct took over.

Her frozen limbs kept her immobilized, unable to fight the shroud, unable to flee the icy dungeon. What could she do if she had her faculties working with her? The locked freezer door was at her feet and there was no room to turn around. Even at her best, she was sealed into what would be her tomb.

And she hadn't been at her best for years. By confining her here, Dr. Darkland had won the battles and the war.

"It took hours for me to finally suffocate," Rochelle said as she took the swept the visions away with ease. "Or maybe my heart stopped. I don't know. All I know is that when the door clanged shut, the sedation drugs had completely worn off and I was left alive and alone. To endure. In hell."

Addie was trembling. Rochelle was gone.

They're evil. The Darkland docs are the purest form of evil.

Something squirmed in her stomach. "Okay Rochelle," she whispered. The light flickered again. "I've got to get them out of here."

CHAPTER NINE

It's Over

Addie's mind raced as she plodded back in the direction of their houseguests. Every fiber of her being wanted to call the police and report their crimes. Their crimes against humanity. Their crimes against Rochelle.

But who would believe you? Your only proof is the memories of a ghost who is afraid of the dark.

Addie stopped at the end of the hall and sucked in a deep breath.

"Here," Marjorie's voice trilled. It echoed off the concrete walls and a certain tone in the word caught Addie's attention. "I brought some cookies as a housewarming present. They're my own special recipe. Here, take one." Her sweet tone darkened. "Each of you."

Addie's eyes widened and she blew out the breath she'd been holding in a huff.

They're poisoned. Like Rochelle's water.

"No cookies before dinner," she called in a voice too high-pitched to be her own. As she stepped into their living room, Tim's hand was poised to take a cookie.

Panic squeezed her words from her throat. "Tim, don't!"

Everyone froze. Both doctors and Tim swiveled their heads and stared at her as though she'd lost her mind. From the recliner, Michaela's indifferent face broke into a grim smile.

Addie straightened her spine and smiled sweetly. "The weatherman said the storm is about to get worse. We're actually under a tornado watch." She strode over and stood behind the couch. "The Darkland docs need to be getting back to their hotel."

She cast a sideways glance at Michaela and prayed she picked up on the hidden message in her word choice.

Michaela nodded and stood up. "Well. Bye."

Tim wore a look of confusion. "Um, Addie? Can we talk in the bedroom please?"

Roland and Marjorie exchanged a glance.

"After they leave we can," she answered flatly. "Drive safe, y'all."

Lightning flashed outside and a low rumble of thunder rattled the windows down the length of the house.

"Adelaide!" Tim's voice was incredulous, but she didn't care.

She ignored him. "Michaela, go on to your room, honey. Now."

Michaela stared at her mother and nodded. It was rare that Addie demanded anything. "Yes ma'am." Rudeness was not in her mother's genetic makeup. This display here in their living room? Her mother knew something about the doctors.

"Michaela!"

She jumped.

Addie cocked her head toward Michaela's room. "Go now, honey."

Slowly, Roland grasped Marjorie's bag in his gnarled hand and rose from the floral-patterned loveseat like a zombie rising from the grave. He nudged his smiling wife with her bag. Marjorie sat the Tupperware bowl of cookies neatly atop the coffee table and accepted the odd purse from her husband. He held it at her middle.

From his pocket, Roland produced a collapsible cane. "Excuse me, Tim?"

"Yes?" Tim shot daggers at his wife before he turned his attention back to their guests.

Roland unfolded the cane and raised it high, like the batter of the losing team at the bottom of the ninth. Before Tim realized what was happening, Roland brought the cane down at a hard angle across his face. Blood sprayed the brown suede couch and Tim sank to the floor.

"Run!" Addie shrieked. Michaela lengthened her strides and ran down the long hallway, just ahead of her mother. They skidded together into Michaela's room. Addie slammed the door and fumbled with the thumb lock until it clicked.

"You were right," Addie said with a huff. "Help me scoot your bookshelf over here." Both struggled to catch their breath as they grabbed Michaela's beloved bookshelf. Each shelf was a different color. Baby blue, baby pink, soft green, and yellow.

Bam!

The bedroom door rattled on its hinges.

"Hurry!"

Together, they maneuvered the full bookshelf in front of the recessed door. "Mom, do you have your phone?"

Addie patted her pants pockets. "No."

"What about Dad?" A tear slipped out the side of Michaela's eye and clung to her cheek during its dramatic descent. "We left him."

Addie had her hands on her hips. Still, she was trembling. "Dad can take care of himself. I had to get you out of there."

The closet door fell open with a creak. Addie jerked at the noise.

"Lisette!"

Addie raised an eyebrow. "Huh? Who is Lisette?"

Bam!

The bedroom door rattled again.

"Mom, in here!" Michaela's voice was a hoarse whisper as she flung open the closet door.

Another crack of lightning outside gave the curtainless room a nuclear glow. Then, the lights went out again.

Lisette glowed against the black of the closet. Her eyes were black, emotionless orbs. She held out her arms like a toddler. Addie choked back a gasp. "What tha—"

"*Mon ami,*" Michaela whispered as rushed in. "Come on Mom, we'll be safe in here. Trust me."

Bang!

The door gave a hideous crack.

"They're coming!" Michaela cried from beside her resident ghost.

Still, Lisette held out her arms. "You are safe with me." Her words were off-key in an unearthly tone.

Addie made a dive for the closet as the bookshelf fell over, just where she'd been standing. Another flash of lightning illuminated the room. Marjorie Darkland stood in the doorway, brandishing Addie's favorite Chinese vase.

Instead of trying to scramble in, Addie slammed the closet doors shut. *Michaela's safe. That's all that matters.*

Marjorie lunged for her, but Addie dodged.

Michaela always keeps a flashlight under her pillow.

Swoosh. Marjorie swung the heavy vase but missed. It crashed into the wooden floor.

Addie fell to her knees and plunged her hand beneath Michaela's pillow. Thankfully, her fingers closed around the skinny mag-light she'd won at school in Dallas. *The Bright Child award.* Addie turned the end of the light and it blazed to life, just as Marjorie flung open the closet door.

"No!"

Addie hit her like a linebacker from behind. The little flashlight clattered to the ground. In the darkness, Marjorie and Addie crashed against the back wall of Michaela's closet. The little mag-light spun a complete circle before coming to rest pointed straight at them.

"Michaela, run," Addie shrieked. She struggled to hold the wiry old woman's arms still. "Michaela?"

She searched the shadowed closet. It was empty.

Something stabbed her leg.

Addie kicked out reflexively. "Ow!"

"Umph," grunted a masculine voice.

"Get her, Roland," Marjorie managed.

Addie kicked out again and landed a solid blow to a soft part of her attacker. She let go of Marjorie and scampered across the floor. She reached down discovered something sticking out of her leg.

A syringe.

She yanked it out.

Michaela isn't in here. Her heart pounded in her ears. *I've got to get out.*

Marjorie struggled onto all fours in the closet and Roland's was lying between her and the door. Addie backed up to the wall and got a running start. *I've got to jump over him.* Three quick strides and she leapt as high as she could.

Marjorie pointed. "Grab her!"

Roland's bony arm came up for her as she leapt over his legs. His fingers hung on the hem of her pants and set her off balance. She smacked the ground in the dark hallway with a thud.

Addie looked over her shoulder into the faintly illuminated bedroom. Roland's breathing was heavy as he lumbered to his feet.

"Tim," she shrieked. Another flash of lightning illuminated Roland's hulking frame as he started toward her. Her leg burned and a scream strangled in her throat.

Thunk.

Roland fell forward. His head landed on her legs.

"Run Addie," Tim cried. "Run!"

Addie leapt to her feet and dashed blindly through the dark house, her burning leg dragging behind her like a stump. Things behind her crashed and shattered, but she didn't stop. The light from her bathroom no longer flickered but burned like a beacon from her bedroom.

Sure enough, her bathroom was like a lighthouse on a rocky shore. The rest of the house had become the stormy ocean. Addie pulled on the pocket door.

"Crap, painted shut!"

She pulled harder. It didn't budge. "Come on," Addie cried through clenched teeth. The muscles in her back and shoulders quivered as she fought the unforgiving door.

"You can't get away." Marjorie called. Her voice was too loud for comfort. "We will get you Adelaide. All three of you. You and your simple child."

Addie caught a glimpse of Marjorie's reflection in the recessed mirror. "Come on!" She fought the door harder. The pocket latch loosened and came off in her hand. Frustrated tears pooled in her eyes as she slid down the wall. "What do you want?" she screamed.

Marjorie stepped around the corner. She smiled sweetly at the woman crumpled on the floor. "We want our house back, dear."

She held a syringe at ready in her gnarled fingers.

"No!" Addie spat at the old woman.

Marjorie took a step toward her. "No use in fighting. It's so much easier when you don't fight."

Addie looked down at the little gold latch in her hand and scrambled to her feet. Out of ideas, she slipped it back into place on the door and yanked hard in a last-ditch effort to save herself. Marjorie dashed forward with the syringe pointed toward her like a bayonet.

Addie's arm popped as the door ripped free of its painted prison and formed a barricade between her and Marjorie. Just in time.

"You only have a moment." Rochelle's voice was a hoarse whisper. "Quickly. Into the hamper."

Addie took a step toward the hamper but froze.

"I have to find Michaela."

"She's safe with Lisette. Trust me."

The bathroom door scooted along its track with a squeal. Rochelle slammed it shut.

"Hurry, Adelaide."

Addie hesitated. "I—I can't. I'm scared, Rochelle." Already, her body was going into panic mode at the thought of stepping into the hamper. The sheer idiocy of being scared of a tiny space more than a syringe-wielding psycho was too ridiculous to think about.

"Get in."

An icy force pushed her backward. Addie's fingers found the cool silver handle and closed around it.

Bang!

The door rattled.

Addie pulled open the hamper. Again, the musty air was a slap in the face.

"Go," Rochelle repeated. Then, the bathroom light went out.

As Addie stepped into the tiny prison, the pocket door flew open.

"Come here!" Marjorie shrieked.

In that instant, the light blazed back to life, brighter than ever before. Rochelle animated before the very doctor who had a hand in making her a ghost. In the hideousness she'd been reduced to, Rochelle reenacted her final moments on earth.

Jerking. Twitching. Blood dripping from her scalp. Screaming for help that would never come. Her chest drew inward as she suffocated, and her fingers clawed at nothing, at anything.

Marjorie screeched and stumbled backward as Addie let the hamper door seal out the last of the brightest light.

Everything around her began to spin.

Calm down, Addie. It's going to be okay. It's going to be okay.

Chilled sweat on her hot skin turned her stomach. Her chest tightened around her pounding heart.

You're alone and stuck in a tiny space. The air is growing thin. You're not going to make it out.

A sudden tremble shook her body and forced her back against the back panel of the tiny space. It creaked, and then let go.

Addie was falling—no, not falling. She was *sliding*. The musty smell was everywhere, but the overwhelming heat gave way to a noticeably cooler temperature. Still, her chest was much too tight and this slide was steep. Before Addie had a chance to realize what was happening, she landed with a tumble in a sandy pit.

She lay there, her long hair in her face, splayed out like a piece of roadkill. Her breathing slowed and her pounding heart did the same. In the darkness, her soft breath came quieter. That was when she realized that she wasn't alone.

CHAPTER 10

RITCHIE'S REVENGE

Tim raised the steel toe work boot high over his head. In their blind rush for Michaela's room, neither of the Darkland doctors knew he was there. Addie leapt over Roland, but he caught the hem of her jeans and she tumbled to the floor.

Smack!

The breath in her lungs whooshed from her body in a sharp huff. Lightning flashed, illuminating the sickening scene. Roland Darkland had a syringe in his hand.

Roland drew his arm back as though he meant to stab it straight through Addie's leg.

"Tim," his wife screamed.

Tim stepped from the obscure hallway and brought the heavy boot down hard on the old man's back.

"Umph." Roland Darkland's lanky frame sunk to the floor.

"Run Addie," Tim cried. "Run!"

The sound of his wife's escape allowed Tim to draw an easy breath despite the darkness. He started after her. Lightning flashed again as Addie turned down the hallway to their bedroom.

Before Tim could join her, something hit him in the head. A final thought filled his mind as an unwelcome burst of stars filled his vision.

The mag light.

The urge to sink to his knees was strong, but Tim clung to the wall.

If I go down, I'll never get up again.

He stumbled forward on weak legs and held his head with one hand. Roland roared behind him.

He's coming in for the kill.

The thought of the mystery syringe and how the cold metal would feel stabbing into his skin propelled him forward.

A scene from *Rikki-Tikki-Tavi*, Michaela's favorite cartoon, filled his mind. The female tailor bird, pretending to be injured, flittered away from Nagaina, a deadly king cobra, down a dirt path.

What's the use in running away, Nagaina hissed in the Kipling classic. *I'm sure to catch you.*

Probably what I look like now.

Roland and Marjorie were the deadly pair of cobras. *Struggling is futile.*

Where's the savior mongoose when you need one?

The thoughts swirled together in Tim's mind as all the doors in the house began to slam.

Bam.

Bam.

Bam! Bam! Bam!

Seizing his chance, Tim pushed off the wall and lengthened his strides down the hall in the direction Addie had gone.

God help me. God help my family.

There was no way to know who—or what—was behind him given the absolute darkness, but his sixth sense told him the venomous doctors were tracking him. He was a wounded gazelle and they were the rabid hyenas.

Tim quieted his breathing as he made his way down the hall.

If I can just find Addie ...

The stench of Old Spice brought him to a halt as a flash of lightning illuminated a bear of a man before him. Tim's eyes widened. The man's face contorted in hard planes that made him appear more monster than man. And his clothes. Varying shades of browns and tans told Tim right away that it was a military uniform.

The door to the safe room, the one where Addie had her fit the day they looked at this house of madness, flew open with such force that it banged into the concrete wall behind it.

"In here, Tim." The strange man's voice had an otherworldly quality. He pointed into the safe room. "Now."

Tim did as he was ordered.

As soon as Tim stepped inside, the door banged shut. "Your wife is safe. She's with Rochelle."

Tim stared at the slightly illuminated figure that stood before him. "You're not real. This isn't real. Who is Rochelle?"

Bang!

The metal door hummed.

"I'm Ritchie." He leaned so close that Tim's eyes crossed. "And it doesn't matter what's real. Those doctors are *real*. And their very *real* goal, their *only* goal for coming here, is to make sure you and your family *cease* to be real. Got it?"

"Where's my daughter, Ritchie?"

Bang!

"She's with Lisette. Also safe." Ritchie clapped his hands and the recessed light in the ceiling buzzed to life.

Tim's voice was soft. "But there can't be light. The storm knocked out the electricity."

"Yes it did." Ritchie dismissed Tim's concerns. "The electric company is not the only source of power in this room, Tim. But more to the point, Roland Darkland owned this house. He knows what it takes to break down that door. You don't have much time. Listen to me very carefully."

Tim nodded. Not only had he not believed in ghosts up until now, but he didn't have time to question everything he thought he knew. "What do you want me to do?"

"Open the box."

Tim looked around. His gaze centered on the built-in box on the floor, the one that was painted and nailed shut.

"It's the only thing in this house I can't open," Ritchie moaned. "Open it now."

"I don't know how to—"

Bang!

The metal door dented in.

"Figure it out. Then, I'll show you the secret exit."

Tim looked down at his boots. He drew back and kicked the little white box. Nothing happened.

Bang!

Tim looked at the dimpled door.

"Again," commanded Ritchie.

Tim kicked hard. Nothing.

Bang!

"Ignore the door," Ritchie shouted. "Again!"

Tim drew up his foot and stomped hard on the top of the box. His boot went straight through.

"Look inside. You have about 30 seconds."

Tim reached in. "Um, key with some numbers on it. Oh, and a pair of silver wedding rings."

Bang!

The head of a sledge hammer came through the metal door.

"You found the wedding rings the Darkland doctors stole from my wife and me. After they murdered us both in cold blood. Take everything in that box and follow me."

Ritchie floated to the back of the safe room while Tim filled his pockets.

Nine … eight … seven …

"Come on. Lean here, Tim. Lean hard."

Roland's arm snaked through the sledgehammer hole and batted at the knobs.

Six … five … four …

Tim did as he was told. He threw his weight against the wall, leaning into his shoulder like he was back on the football field in his glory days.

Three … two … one.

Click.

The door to the safe room flew open and Roland stepped in.

The wall to the secret exit opened inward. Roland raised the sledgehammer, but Ritchie was waiting. Every cabinet door in the safe room began to bang.

Open, shut, open, shut. Faster, faster! Roland dropped his weapon and flung his hands over his ears and ran from the room.

"Go!" Ritchie demanded. Tim leapt into the newly dis-covered darkness. Down he fell. His stomach leapt during the free fall and, for a moment, Tim feared he may puke. He hit something—a slide maybe—at an angle and slid down at record speed. A moment later, his face ground into soft dirt.

"Uhh," he groaned.

Tim opened his eyes, but it didn't matter. He was cloaked

in absolute darkness. He patted the pockets of his jeans. The wedding rings and the key were still in their places.

This stuff must be pretty important if it's worth killing over.

When his head stopped buzzing, somebody's soft breathing harmonized with his. The tiny hairs on the back of his neck rose like hackles.

I'm not alone in here.

CHAPTER ELEVEN

Lisette's Realization

"Where are we ... how did we ..." Michaela's tongue threatened to tie itself in a knot as she looked around at their surroundings. Scenic Mountain rose up to their immediate right. From here, Michaela couldn't see the road or anything else that looked remotely civilized.

She took a step toward where her house should be. The toe of her tennis shoe banged against something metal. "Ow."

Michaela squatted down to examine what she'd accidentally discovered. As her eyes adjusted to the darkness, she spied the spiked wrought iron fence that wouldn't have looked new a hundred years ago. Slowly, she turned. The fence formed a small rectangle, and she was inside.

Weeds and tall grasses, still heavy with wetness from the passing storm, towered up and over the rusted posts, nearly obscuring it.

"I promised your *mamah* I would keep you safe," Lisette's voice tolled in the darkness like a church bell at a funeral service. "And so I am."

Michaela tilted her face and studied her slightly illuminated friend. "But how did we get *here*? From the house?"

Lisette shrugged. A glow the color of starlight faintly trailed her shoulders when they moved.

Somewhere, Michaela could hear panting. "Is Dog here, too?"

Lisette nodded. The same ghostly trail followed even the slightest of her movements. "I do not know how we got here. I just hugged you and wished really hard to be here and not in the house. And here we are."

Her visage flickered in the moonlight, like a light bulb about to wink out.

Michaela looked deeper into the shadowed grass between them. Gray markers peeked up from between the oversized dandelion puffs.

Michaela's mind wandered back to the first time she found Lisette here at the base of Scenic Mountain, on their first day in the new house.

"Lisette!" She'd called. "Lisette?"

No answer.

Michaela stepped into the closet but found it empty; she was alone in the darkness. Her friend was gone.

She strode through the house, careful to stay away from the opening to the attic. Ritchie was up there somewhere, and Lisette had already schooled her on his meanness.

Michaela stepped quietly down the hall. The light from Mom's writing nook was a pale yellow glow on the hallway tile. She was reading something out loud in quiet mumbles. From what it sounded like, another publisher had turned down ***A Heart on Hold***. Her shoulders sagged a bit for her mother. Dad would be home from the store any minute now.

Michaela crept through the living room and into the kitchen and pushed open the front door. A chilled whoosh of air sucked it shut behind her.

The sun was sinking fast in the west and the yard was an

ever changing palette of pastels. Scenic Mountain loomed behind the house. Something about it beckoned Michaela toward it. With her strides lengthening, Michaela let the distance between her and her new home grow.

She paused a moment at the highway and looked both ways, just like her parents taught her. A semi flicked on its headlights as it roared past. As it screamed into the falling darkness, Michaela found herself alone again on the side of the empty road. A pair of cardinals called out from her backyard and their *wheep wheep wheep* echoed in the tiny valley. Michaela was completely alone.

Her heart thundered in her chest and her mouth went dry as she looked both ways again. She sucked in a deep breath and dashed across the empty street.

Thorns scratched at her legs as she trudged around the base of Scenic Mountain. "Lisette?" she called quietly.

Why not yell louder? There's no one to hear.

Still, Michaela glanced over her shoulder. Her house grew smaller until it disappeared. Deep blue shadows hugged the far side of the mountain, but still she turned back and continued her hike.

Just a little bit further.

A flash of gray caught her eye. "Lisette!"

The gauzy figure turned its pale face toward her. Its dark eyes were empty. Michaela's breath caught in her throat. "Lisette, is it you?"

"Michaela, you shouldn't have come here." The figure hovered just a few strides away, but the voice sounded hundreds of years apart from her.

Michaela grinned. "I missed you. And we're best friends, remember?" Before Michaela could close the gap between them, something rattled in the dry leaves beneath the thorny mesquite beside her. She froze.

Rattlesnake.

"Don't move," Lisette commanded. She was at Michaela's side in a moment.

Michaela dared a peek down. The deadly viper was curled into an S-shape, with his head off the ground. Should he strike, he was so close that he could hit her before she could even step away. The breeze from the snake's rattle in the grass met her bare ankle and a chilly film of sweat cropped up across her upper lip.

Lisette's voice was a harsh echo. "When I say move, you move. Don't look back, just run straight ahead. Run for your life."

Michaela nodded, careful to keep her feet still as stone.

"Get ready," Lisette's hollow voice commanded. "Get set ..."

A trickle of pebbles made the rattler's tail speed up in the dead leaves. Michaela squeezed her eyes shut.

"Go! Go Michaela, go!"

With her eyes still closed, Michaela ignored the deafening sound behind her and did as she was told. She ran for her life across the dark, dangerous field.

After an eternity of moments, Michaela slowed to a stop and dared to turn around. A pile of rocks from the overhang rested where the rattler had been moments before. Michaela put her hands on her knees and sucked in deep breaths. Her mother's voice was loud in her head.

In through your nose, out through your mouth.

She kicked an out-of-place pebble. Something clanged.

Intrigued, Michaela pulled herself upright and swept the tall prairie grass aside. It wasn't a pebble she'd kicked; it was a piece of rusted-out wrought iron. And it was still stuck in the ground. Before she could investigate further, a chilled breeze met the back of her neck.

"There now. Are you all right?" Lisette's voice was smaller, far off, and Michaela couldn't see her anymore.

She turned her attention away from the wrought iron. "Yes, thank you. Hey, where are you?" Michaela turned in a full circle, but the only thing she saw was the bright silver moon creeping higher into the sky. The sun was full set and her mom would be looking for her, frantic no doubt.

"I'm here. That made me tired, Michaela. I'm not supposed to do stuff like that, but you were going to get bitten. I had to push the rocks."

Michaela noticed more wrought iron poking up from the weeds and grass. She stepped toward it. "I know. Thanks. And I'm not even scared of snakes."

"I am."

She put her hands on the small fence, half-overgrown and almost entirely invisible if you weren't looking for it. "What are you doing out here, anyway?"

"I don't really know. I like to come here sometimes when I'm sad."

"Why?"

"I don't know. I just sit in that little fence and after a while I feel better." Lisette's voice was as cold and distant as the stars. "But it's time to go back. She is probably scared."

Michaela puzzled over the words. "Who is she?"

"The girl in the closet with me."

Lisette's musical voice drifted toward the house, so Michaela ignored the icy prickles that made the little hairs on the back of her neck stand on end and followed her. "I thought you were alone in my closet?"

"I was until your family got all moved in. Then she came."

Michaela didn't look at the pile of rocks that covered the snake. Instead, she focused on the darkness that stretched out before her. She wasn't scared with her friend nearby, even if she couldn't see her. Still, bubbles of jealousy rose in her stomach. If Lisette had another ghost to live in the closet with her, she may not want to be best friends anymore. "Is she, well, nice?"

"*Oui*. Young, so very young."

Michaela shook her head and cleared the foggy memory away. It felt like a lifetime ago. Lisette was staring at her.

"Um, what did you say?"

Lisette smiled. "I said, you have so many questions and I have no answers for you. All I can tell you is that I come here when I am scared. I do not know why, but I feel safe here."

"Are my mom and dad going to be okay, Lisette?"

Lisette shrugged. "Good usually wins over evil. But not always."

Michaela's heart sank. She pushed the grasses to the side and traced one finger along the old carved words.

Gerard St. Clair

B— Abt. 1850, Burgundy France

D – 1892, Big Spring Texas

Volé par des bandits et laissé pour mort

Dieu ait son âme

Michaela's breath caught in her throat. She moved to the next marker.

Aimee St. Clair
B – Abt. 1860, Burgundy France
D – 1892, Big Spring Texas
Volé par des bandits et laissé pour mort
Dieu ait son âme

Tears shimmered in Michaela's eyes. Lisette looked on, her own dark eyes like flecks of coal in the moonlight. "*Mon ami?* What is the matter?"

Michaela stared at her, her lower lip trembling. "Lisette, is your last name St. Claire?"

Lisette sat in front of the third and the smallest marker. She nonchalantly twirled a bright yellow flower on its stem. "*Oui*, how did you know?"

Michaela squeezed her eyes shut. A tear eked out and dripped down her cheek.

How do I tell my best friend that she is sitting on her own grave?

"Can you read the words on the marker behind you, Lisette?"

Michaela pushed herself up onto her knees and chose her words carefully. She could see through her friend and almost make out the words from where she sat on the muddy earth.

Lisette shrugged again. "I tried once. No, not once. I have tried lots of times." Her face was paler than usual. "But I can't read the English."

Taking care to keep her voice gentle, Michaela peered through Lisette. She inched over to the small stone.

"Look here." She traced the words with her finger as she read.

Lisette St. Clair.
Born 1884
Died 1892
avec son chien.
At the last it bites like a serpent and stings like a viper.
Proverbs 23:32

Lisette's mouth hung agape and she turned to look at the stone. "This is my grave? And Dog's?"

"If that is what the French says, then yes. Yours and Dog's," Michaela agreed. She pointed to the other two markers. "These are your parents' graves. I can't read the French on them though." She fumbled her tongue around the French words as best as she could.

Lisette hung her head. "It says they were held up by highwaymen. And killed. And for God to rest please their souls." Emotion roiled out from the young phantom in billowy, echoing sobs that sounded akin to nails on a chalkboard.

Michaela's heart broke for her friend.

"Even if I had held on, if I had gotten Dog to hold on. They never would have come for me anyway. And still, here I wait."

Michaela looked off into the distance. "I guess we'll both sit here and wait for our parents, for as long as it takes them to find us."

CHAPTER TWELVE

BIG SPRING SANATORIUM

In the dank, musty darkness, a light flickered to life. Addie fought to focus on the figure it illuminated. She squinted into the darkness and prepared herself to run, bum leg or not. Or to fight.

"Hello Adelaide."

Addie's jaw went slack. "Tim, oh Tim!"

She dug her fingers into the soft dirt and pulled herself across the sandy pit. Tim smiled at her. She threw her arms around her husband's neck and the sobs roiled up from the pit of her very being. "I'm so glad you kept that stupid cigarette lighter."

"Does that mean it's a good thing that I don't always do what you say?" He nuzzled her neck and hair and held her tight. "Are you all right?"

"Yes." Addie nodded and swiped the watery emotion from her eyes. "They stabbed me with that needle. It burned."

Tim knelt to examine her wound. "Right here?" He touched her leg.

Addie winced. "Yes. I don't think they injected anything though."

"It's swollen," Tim confirmed. "Can you bear weight on it?"

She stood on both feet and nodded. "It's uncomfortable, but I can. A little."

"Good."

Tim stood up and relit the little green lighter. "Where are we, Addie?"

He held it high above his head while Addie examined their surroundings. "Well, it looks like we are in some sort of old, fortified bunker. There used to be an airfield here ..." She hummed as she thought. "Lester Army Airfield; that's it. It was active during World War II, then shut down. This must have been the *rendezvous* point in case the Axis Powers got the upper hand."

She looked at Tim. "Bunkers at that time were built into mountains. Like NORAD in Colorado."

Tim followed his wife's train of thought. "We're inside of Scenic Mountain, aren't we?"

Addie didn't answer but limped toward the far wall. "Wooden boxes marked TNT." She lifted the lid. "Nothing in here though."

Tim looked around. "In that corner over there, it looks like a bunch of canteens. Army canteens."

Addie nodded and flexed her leg. Before she could speak, something caught her eye. "Look, Tim. There!"

She pointed to the wall that had been behind them. "There's a sign. And that's definitely been put up since the war ended."

Tim held out his hand to her and pulled her to her feet. They trudged through the thick sand to get a closer look. "This is where the musty smell in the hamper came from," Addie muttered.

"You got here through the hamper?" Tim looked incredulous. "I got here through the safe room next to your writing nook."

They shared a smile before turning their attention back to the sign.

Tim read aloud. "Big Spring Sanatorium. Then an arrow pointing straight ahead."

"A secret passage from the house to the asylum." She squeezed his arm. "I guess we know where we are supposed to go."

Tim extinguished the light and they started down the cramped, dark hall together in comfortable silence. Addie let her hand trail along the packed dirt wall.

Finally, Tim broke the silence. "I'm sorry I said that about you needing to talk to someone, professionally I mean." His voice was a whisper.

Addie reached through the thick darkness and caught her husband's hand. "That's okay. Honestly, I was beginning to wonder if I wasn't going off the deep end. What with seeing Rochelle in the bathroom, then Lisette in Michaela's closet."

Adelaide's words hung suspended in the dank air. Tim relit the lighter. It took several tries, but it finally flamed to life.

"You've known about this since before today? I mean the supernatural element in the—what did Michaela name it— The House of Madness?"

Addie couldn't look at him as she trudged through the sand. "Yes."

"Why didn't you tell me?" After a moment, Tim answered himself. "Never mind, I already know the answer to that. I wouldn't have told me, either."

They shared a quiet giggle as the passage narrowed.

"We're probably getting close," Addie whispered under her breath. "Hey, what did you see to make you believe?"

Tim sighed. The look on his face said he wasn't entirely

sure he believed what he was about to say. "After you got away from the docs, they came after me. Roland hit me with Michaela's mag light, so I wasn't at the top of my game. A man, a soldier I guess, showed me how to get out of the house. The secret exit in that safe room I mentioned."

The trail slanted upward. Addie cut her eyes to her husband. "I haven't seen him."

"Do you remember the painted-shut box in that safe room?"

"Mm-hmm."

Tim continued. "Well, he made me break into it."

Addie's voice was low. "Made you?"

Tim exhaled a huff. "It doesn't really make sense, but then, it makes perfect sense. And, it's hard to explain. There was a sledge hammer involved."

Addie snorted. "Did you find anything? In the box, I mean."

"Actually, yes." Tim patted his pocket with his free hand. "There was a pair of wedding rings that Ritchie, the solider ghost, said belonged to him and his wife. And an old key."

Tim stopped walking and pulled the key with the numbers out of his pocket. He pressed it into Addie's hand and held the lighter close. The tunnel's slope took a steep upward slant, so much that they were going to have to climb it on their hands and knees.

"Did Ritchie say what the key was?"

"No." Tim took the key back and stuffed it down in his pocket before scrambling up the steepest part of the trail. Somehow, he managed to keep the lighter lit.

"Isn't that burning your thumb?" Addie asked.

"I'm tough," he winked. Tim offered his free hand to help Addie up onto the ledge. "He didn't say anything. But for the Darklands to come back and try to kill us ..." His voice trailed off into the darkness. He let the light extinguish. "Well, maybe my thumb did burn a little."

Addie felt for the lighter in Tim's hand and lit it. The metal end was molten hot. "We're here." She pointed to the wall they'd reached. An unobtrusive door was there. Waiting. She and Tim shared a glance. "Maybe there'll be more answers on the other side."

Tim tried the knob. The door opened easily.

"Is it weird that this wasn't locked?"

Tim shrugged. "I don't know why it would be locked, being the only entrance from a secret passage."

"True." Addie looked around the muted room. The earthen floor was lumpy and scattered papers proved to be an odd, thick carpet. The rank smell of mildew assaulted her nose and brought water to her eyes. A cabinet marked Emergency Supplies leaned dtrunkenly against the far wall, its doors hanging open. Inside was an empty first aid kit, what appeared to be a stock of dehydrated foods, and an old Coleman lantern with a sealed gallon can of white gas.

"And people say there is no God," Addie quipped.

"My grandfather used one of these when he took me fishing when I was a kid," Tim marveled. "I wonder if it still works?"

Tim filled the lantern's fuel chamber, released the pressure plunger, pumped it a dozen times, then locked it back into place. He pulled up the glass and tied the mantles to the gas tubes. "Moment of truth," he said. "Hope this thing doesn't blow up in my face."

Addie gave him a grim nod, and Tim held the lighter beneath the mantles, and the instantly caught fire. A grin spread across Tim's face. "Just like riding a bike," he said.

Tim finished prepping the lantern, which was now casting a cheery glow into their eerie surroundings. "Look, on the back of the door," Tim pointed. Another sign."

"To Scenic Mountain Bunker." Addie looked at her husband. "You were right. We were *inside* the mountain."

"No wonder that dang slide was so long." Tim kicked a paper. "So where are we now?"

Addie leaned and plucked a moldy paper from the floor. "It's a basement," she surmised. "And this is a paper from a medical chart." She skimmed it before dropping it back onto the floor. "And the sign in the bunker was right. We're *underneath* Big Spring Sanatorium."

The horrific scenes Rochelle showed her pushed their way to the forefront of Addie's adrenaline-charged mind. So much so, that she was almost overcome with emotion as she glanced around.

Filing cabinets lay on their sides, the drawers pulled out and emptied of their contents. An old wheelchair, missing a front wheel, sat in the corner and wore a thick layer of dirt. Toppled IV poles and hospital gowns made a checkered mess across the floor. A giant box, decaying against the wall, looked large enough to hold a refrigerator. Scrawled on the side in permanent marker were the words HARD RESTRAINTS.

Addie drew her fist to her mouth. It smelled of mildew, so she dropped it. "Oh Tim, those doctors did horrible things here."

Tim let out a long, even breath. "Well, maybe if we can find what this key goes to, we can prove that fact. And those doctors will have to trade in their Jamaican condo for a jail cell." He pulled the key from his pocket.

DBL – 4

"May as well try and crack this code." Tim looked at Addie. "What do you make of it, Miss Author Teacher?

"Make that Mrs." Addie forced a polite smile and took the key. "It's small, like a filing cabinet key." She glanced around. "See if we can match it to these filing cabinets here."

Tim and Addie separated in the dim light and began studying the toppled cabinets. Addie tilted her head to read the letters and numbers. "This one says patient files, A-C," she relayed. "I have M-O, here. Same thing."

On a hunch, Addie plucked up a fistful of the moldy papers and sat down on the makeshift gray bench. "Maybe we'll get lucky and find our incriminating papers just lying around." She studied them in the low light.

"Found D-F," Tim relayed. "Are you having any luck?"

Addie shook her head slowly. "No, none. These are all old patient files. And they look legit. With release dates and family member phone numbers." She set the papers beside her on the filing cabinet seat. "I think the stuff that is in whatever box that key goes to won't have any release dates." She dropped her voice to a whisper. "Rochelle certainly wasn't released."

Tim took out the key again. "Here, let's think this through. What could this number mean?"

Addie took the tiny brass key from Tim's palm and turned it this way and that. "Well, the number is four. Doesn't this place have four floors?"

"Yes," Tim said. "Because Michaela counted the boarded-up windows when we passed it the other day. Remember?"

"Yup." Addie managed to get to her feet. Her leg throbbed. "So, let's try the fourth floor first."

"Sounds good to me." Tim plucked up a lantern and held it gingerly, as though he'd plucked a rotten carrot from a garden wasteland. "I suggest we take the stairs. Something tells me the elevators are out of order."

Tim and Addie found the stairs easily. A thick layer of grime covered the them, like a furry brown coat.

"I hope nobody tries to follow us, we're leaving a perfect trail." Addie pointed to her bare footprint in the grime. "I wish I had some shoes on. This is gross."

Tim waved the light like a train conductor from years gone by. "There's the ground floor."

They trudged up the stairs, hand in hand, their soft breath accenting the steep climb. Finally, Tim's voice broke the silence. "Like I was saying back in the tunnel. I'm sorry, Addie."

"Sorry for what?" With her free hand, Adelaide gripped her leg. The throbs were receding, but it still hurt.

It wasn't until they passed the landing for the second floor that Tim spoke again. "About baby Juliette. I wasn't the best husband, or a very good friend."

"Oh." *Please, not now. I can't go back there right now.*

Still, Tim continued, choosing his words carefully. "I guess it just hurt so bad. I was stupid and let myself take it out on you. Which was wrong. I'm really sorry."

Addie stopped climbing and opened her mouth to speak. Tim put his finger to her lips. "You don't have to say anything."

He pulled her close, right there in the unnerving dark of the back stairwell in Big Spring Sanatorium. Ever slow, he tilted his wife's chin upward and erased the space between them. As their lips met, a wayward sound made them freeze.

"They have to be here somewhere," a muffled voice reasoned.

Adelaide recognized the nasal voice in an instant. "That's Marjorie."

A masculine voice answered. "We'll get them. They can't get away."

"Roland," Tim agreed. "Come on, to the fourth floor."

Tim let his hand trail down his Addie's arm, just like when they were dating so many years ago. Their hands caught, and Tim raced up the stairs, pulling Addie along behind him.

Addie pressed gently on the metal door with the black number four on it. "Good thing, because the stairs dead ended into this floor."

"The top floor," Tim agreed. "We better stick something in here. Just in case it locks behind us."

Addie nodded and pushed the door the rest of the way open. Thankfully, it didn't squeak. Tim held the lantern out before them. The sight was enough to take Addie's breath. Papers carpeted the filthy ground, just as they had in the basement, and an odd smell surrounded them.

"Smells like formaldehyde and ... chlorine bleach," Tim said, reading her mind.

"Yeah. Gross." Addie gingerly picked up a molded manila folder and stuck it over the lock before letting the door fall back into place. "Let's see, do you see anything that would need a key to open it?"

"Maybe at the nurses' station?" Tim picked his way across the open floor, careful not to touch the strap-back wheelchairs or glass bottle IV stands. "It looks like a bomb went off in here."

Addie peeked into a room as they went by. The windows were boarded up, but the light from Tim's lantern illuminated the entrails of the semi-private room. A pair of candy-cane stirrups protruded off the end of the bed and a smashed baby warmer sat in the corner beneath a thick layer of dust. Hard restraints, the kind with the buckles, dangled from the bed rails.

"What is this place?"

Tim already made his way to the nurse's station. He held up a three-ring binder. "It's the mother-baby unit."

Addie sucked in her lower lip and chewed. *If the Darkland doctors were so cruel to the adult patients …*

Stop. She couldn't think of the horrors that took place here. And to mothers, out of their minds with pain and mental illness, *or postpartum depression*, and the voiceless, helpless creatures that didn't ask to be brought into this world.

There are hard restraints hanging from the bed. The mothers were restrained while they gave birth.

Hot bile surged in Addie's throat and threatened to choke her. For a moment, she saw a flash of herself lying that bed, restrained. Screaming Juliette's name.

Did they put depressed mothers of miscarried babies here, too?

"Found it," Tim announced. "There's a file cabinet. And it looks like it matches …"

Addie tore her gaze away from the room. *That could have been me in there.*

"Wait, false alarm. ABL – 4." The excited note disappeared from Tim's voice. Still, he continued. "I think all of these at the nurse's stations will end in four. It's the first letter that changes."

"A for Antepartum, maybe?" Emotion strained Addie's words. The image of her dead baby and her black, bubbly skin burned in her mind.

A voice hissed like a serpent in her ear. *Get out of here, Addie.*

She closed her eyes and whispered so that Tim couldn't hear. "Is someone there?"

The voice came again. *Now.*

Icy prickles slithered down Addie's neck and made her shiver. She opened her eyes, but nobody was there. Only Tim at the nurse's station.

The metal double doors at the far end of the unit squeaked to life.

Tim's stopped rummaging and his voice escaped his lips in a strangled whisper. "It's them!"

Addie ducked into the room and peeked from behind the wall. "Can we make it back to the stairs?"

Tim nodded. "One way to find out."

Adelaide sniffed and fought the urge to look over her shoulder at the horrific bed that loomed behind her like the monster in her closet when she was a girl. She pretended the moisture in her eyes was brought on from the hideous smell. The sound of a crying infant, far away, met her ears.

Beams from Marjorie and Roland's flashlights danced over the filthy floor, just around the corner. They disappeared for a moment, then reappeared.

They're searching the rooms.

Addie crept out of the room and stepped carefully over a stack of files that appeared to have been tossed hard from out of a filing cabinet, but the heart-wrenching cry wouldn't be stifled. "Just feed the baby. He's hungry. Just feed him. Somebody. Anybody."

How do you know it's a him?

"Addie? Are you talking to me?" Tim didn't wait for an answer as he took the less careful approach. "Come on."

He made it to the door in three strides. Addie slunk out

behind him. The sound of the wailing infant grew distant behind her.

He pushed it open and let the manila envelope fall to the floor. "We have to get to the third floor before they do. We do want to go there next, right?"

When they were safely on the landing, Addie replied. "I guess so. I don't understand their system at all."

Flashlight beams flashed through the glass window on the door.

"Duck!" Tim pulled her down. "Do you think they saw us?"

Addie kept her voice low. "I don't want to stick around and find out. Come on!" She tried to step in her same footprints on the way to the third floor, but the closer they got to the third floor, the more careless she became.

A metallic groan from the metal door above them met Addie's ears.

"There are footprints. Roland! They went this way!"

Addie grabbed Tim's arm. "They know we're here."

Tim jumped down the last two steps and opened the door. "Then we'll just have to be faster than they are." Together, they dashed through the third-floor door.

Addie didn't bother to peer into the rooms on this floor, partly because she was running and partly because there were no rooms. It was completely open on the third floor, but restraints hung from the walls.

The harsh stench of stale urine made her gag. Addie shivered as Tim slid on his knees behind the desk like a star player sliding for home. Like everywhere else, papers littered the floor. Behind the urine stench, the smell was different. Old. Musty. Heavy with broken hearts.

"PBL – 4," Tim called. "It's a no go,"

"Probably for psychotic," Addie whispered. She stared at the door they'd come through and bounced on her bare feet. "Why aren't they here yet?"

Tim's voice interrupted her thoughts, which were threatening to turn hysteric. "Want to try the second floor, or go straight to the first?"

The back stairway door flew open. "There they are!"

Addie looked at her husband. "I'll go to the first and you take the second. They can't follow both of us."

"And meet in the basement," Tim finished. He leaned forward and brushed Addie's lips with a dry kiss. Their first kiss in so long. "Here, take the lantern. I love you, Addie."

She accepted it. "I love you, too."

They stood up and faced the Darkland doctors. Marjorie still had her syringe and Roland held a straitjacket in front of him.

"Go!" Tim yelled.

Tim ran straight at them with a rebel yell in his throat. Addie headed for the far stairs. Rochelle's story played again and again in her mind.

DBL – 4. DBL – 4.

Addie took the stairs two and three at a time. When she reached the first floor, she didn't hesitate and burst through the double doors, bound for the nurse's station.

They didn't beat me here.

Almost as soon as the words formed in her brain, her foot jerked out from under her. Addie fell hard on the fusty floor and her jaw popped. The lantern skittered away, but stayed on. She pushed herself up and fought to catch her breath. The asylum's deathly stench was even worse nearer the floor.

She tugged on her ankle.

It's a snare!

The more she tugged, the more the rope bit into her bare ankle.

Addie's throat began to tighten.

They set a trap.

Addie glanced around wildly.

A scalpel a scalpel, my kingdom for a scalpel.

She shuffled through the papers, but there was nothing there. Any moment, one of the sets of doors would open and the doctors would be here—either one or both of them.

What if they set a trap on Tim's floor?

Her eyes came to rest on the far wall. Something looked familiar —something in the tilework she hadn't noticed on the other floors.

Then, it hit her.

This is where Rochelle was. Somewhere around here. This must be where they did lobotomies and electro-shock therapy.

Pulsing throbs coursed over Addie's body as she went to work on the rope again. A flash of movement caught her eye. Addie ignored it. She wouldn't sit here and wait for death, she couldn't. Michaela's angelic face appeared in her mind. She would try to escape until she couldn't try anymore.

A metallic scraping broke the heavy quiet. Addie didn't look up.

Probably chains. They'll lock me up in the basement with chains.

Blood seeped from her fingers as she battled the rope.

What kind of knot is this?

The scraping grew steadily louder. And closer.

When it was right behind her, Addie arched her back and waited for the pain. She didn't realize she'd closed her eyes until she opened them. A pair of silver scissors lay beside her.

Addie glanced over her shoulder. A figure, another woman, dragged herself over the papers and across the floor. Her legs were twisted grotesquely and trailed behind her like tentacles. Her long hair hung in mats. The specter looked back at Addie. When its eyes—or what used to be eyes—met Addie's, she gasped. The hideous creature was grinning.

The face was no longer a face, but more of a permanent grimace.

Was her mouth cut? Or sewn shut?

No doubt she was beautiful once, like Rochelle, before this place took her beauty from her. And from the looks of it, her life. "Thank you," Addie rasped.

Like a wine stain on a Monet.

The phantom tried to open her mouth to speak, but only a hideous gurgle came out. Addie shivered as the helpful phantasm dragged herself across the floor and disappeared behind the nurses' station.

Addie snatched up the scissors and hacked at her rope bond.

Finally, free.

She put the scissors down and pushed herself to her feet. The far door creaked open.

Roland ran at her like a freight train, the straitjacket still stretched out before him. Addie leaned and made a grab for the scissors, but only succeeded in sending them skittering across the floor. She stumbled toward the same door she had come in.

I'm sorry Tim, she thought. *I can't check the filing cabinet with them in here.*

Addie pushed on the door. Locked. She tried the other side. Something was stuck on the other side.

I'm trapped!

Marjorie's face appeared in the glass. The old woman fought to get in but succeeded in only opening the door a couple of inches. She wiggled her arm inside and swung and jabbed with her needle. "Get her, Roland!"

The needle caught Addie's skin, but she jerked back. A thin trail of blood followed the syringe down her arm. It flamed at once. "What is *in* that thing," she screamed at Marjorie, who still swung wildly.

She pushed hard on the door. *If I can just knock that old broad down the stairs—*

Ethereal breath tickled Addie's ear. *Kick, Addie. Kick now.*

The thought was so strong in her mind that Addie kicked behind her like a mule. She glanced back in time to see Roland double over.

Finish him.

Addie grasped her hands together and brought them down like a club on his back. Something cracked and he slumped to the floor.

Run!

She didn't look back at Marjorie, who still battled the door, but instead ran for the back stairs. Her bare feet slipped on the sheaves of papers as she ran. Away from the nurses' station. Away from the filing cabinet. Away from the Darkland doctors. And away from her lantern and the lifesaving scissors.

Addie's arm was swollen and throbbing when she skidded out the door and into the dark stairwell.

"Tim please be in the basement. Please," Addie said. She leapt down the stairs. Her back jarred when she landed, and her breath came in hard, sharp gasps.

Addie rounded the last corner, leapt down the last of the

stairs, and landed in a crouch. Stinging pain shot up her bare feet, momentarily immobilizing her. She couldn't wait for the pain to pass, but instead flung herself at the door. It opened easily.

No Tim.

"Tim?" she rasped. Addie held her throbbing arm in one hand. "Tim!"

The door to the bunker burst open. "Addie!"

She stumbled into her husband's waiting arms. "I'm sorry, they almost got me. I couldn't see if our cabinet was on my floor."

"I couldn't check the second floor, either. They had it booby-trapped." He held her tight against his chest.

"I got caught in a snare. Did they catch you, too?"

Tim stroked her hair. "No, I was able to avoid it."

"Then what took you so long?" The words hung up in tears of relief.

Tim held her at arm's length, his hands on her shoulders. "I didn't find the cabinet. But I found so much other stuff. Polaroids of patients restrained in their beds. Pictures of them in the showers with their bones protruding... Addie, these doctors reduced them to living skeletons. Maybe if we turn them in ..."

The odd, hissing voice was back. *Lock the doors.*

The phantom thought itself was powerful enough to propel Addie on its own. "Lock the doors Tim," Adelaide interrupted. "They're coming."

No sooner had Tim locked the deadbolt, then something hit it.

Bam!

Addie eased herself backward. "There's probably another

way in here that only they—" Something caught her ankle and she hit the ground. Her hip exploded in starbursts of pain. "Umph."

Tim rushed to her side. "Addie, what hap—" He looked down.

The letters DBL – 4 stared up at them from a partially buried box.

"Honey, you found it." Tim plunged the key into the lock. It slid open effortlessly. He lifted the lid. Rows of neat files sat undisturbed. "Or it found you."

Addie pulled out a file. Clipped to the front of the manila envelope was a Polaroid snapshot of a striking young woman. With long red hair and big green eyes, she looked out of place in the mysterious box.

Bang!

"What, do they have a collapsible battering ram they carry around, too?" Tim asked.

Addie flipped open the redhead's file.

"Honey, your arm. It's ... green."

"She got me with that needle. Oh my goodness Tim, listen." Addie pointed to a spot on the meticulously handwritten page, just beneath the red stamp that warned DO NOT FILE. MED STUDY. "Lynda Wells, age 23. Preschool Teacher. Body Dysmorphic Disorder. Started med study—"

"Wait," Tim interrupted. "What's that body thing?"

Addie still skimmed the page. "Anorexia and bulimia probably. This beautiful girl thought she was fat. Where was I ..." Addie traced the page with her finger. "Started med study on day two of confinement. Severe reaction to dose ... must lower for people with compromised body function. Muscle tetanus of lower extremities resulting in fractured spine."

The phantom who dragged herself across the floor to give me the scissors.

"She helped me Tim, when I was stuck on the first floor. "That's why she couldn't talk. Her gag reflex ..."

"This is it. This is what they were after." Tim looked at Addie as something hit the door again. "What does D stand for?"

Addie's voice was a whisper. "Dead. Or died."

"Deceased." Tim inched over to the door. "Is it odd they're just hitting the door now, but not trying to get in?" His voice was a harsh whisper.

As soon as he said it, Addie knew they'd been had. "Because it was a distraction."

"Very good," Marjorie said to the tune of a slow clap. "But not good enough."

I knew there was another way in.

She opened the locked door and Roland joined her in her sarcastic round of applause.

"So tell me, how does it feel knowing you gave up everything— your lives, the life of your daughter—all for that box? It will never see the outside of this building, you know. It was all for nothing."

Addie stuck Lynda's file back in the box and shut it. "I'd like to know how you people sleep at night. Look at what you've done. What you're *about* to do. When is enough going to be enough?"

"People know what you did. And those who don't know— they will soon," Tim added.

Marjorie laughed. "And how will anyone know?"

Addie tilted her chin. "Because I'm going to tell them. I'm going to write every single one of their stories and there is nothing you can do to stop me. The truth is stronger than whatever force is driving you." Addie clutched the small box to her chest.

Something flickered behind Marjorie.

The doors on a row of cabinets along the top of the wall opened with a long, slow series of creaks and the faint scent of Old Spice permeated the musty air.

"Roland, put her in the straitjacket."

Addie spun on her heel and faced him. "Rochelle Richardson. Bipolar. Tortured and medicated against her will and without her consent."

Marjorie's jaw went slack.

"Private Ritchie Zambrano. He responded well to your new drug, the one that made you millionaires, didn't he? Then, his wife saw you torturing Rochelle—ripping out her hair from the actual scalp."

Tim shook his head. "You killed her to keep your secret safe, then you had to kill him, too." He stepped to his wife's side. "Now we're leaving."

"You can't leave," Marjorie sputtered. "Get back here with my files!" Her voice rose to nasal level.

"Lynda Wells. How did the poor girl manage to break her back the second day in your care? Be thinking how you want to answer. The authorities will be asking you both that very question."

A metallic click made Addie swallow her words. From the corner of her eye, she saw Roland level his .38 Special at her head.

"We wanted to have a little fun with you," Marjorie said. "Maybe a stimulation experiment, like the kind that drove *Rochelle* more bonkers than she already was. Or maybe test the dosage of this new medicine, you know, the one that *burned like fire*. As it should, since it was mostly carbolic acid. Now give me my files."

Before Roland could pull the trigger, the ground at his feet began to pulsate. "What tha—"

Ghost white fingers sprouted from the dirt like dead daisies. As she pulled herself out of the ground, the cabinet doors began to bang. Not all at once, but one after the other.

Bang, bang, bang!

Roland aimed his gun at the girl who clawed at his legs as she climbed out of her tomb and pulled the trigger.

Click.

He cocked, aimed, and squeezed again.

Click.

Roland screamed as the ghost girl's hands ripped his black pants to ribbons. Her long nails clawed at his exposed flesh, as though she were clawing for her very life.

Marjorie looked wildly over first one shoulder, then the next. Then, the laughing started but did nothing to drown out the incessant banging.

Bangbangbangbangbangbang!

Maniacal laughing came from all corners of the basement as the apparitions began to appear.

Ritchie flashed to life. "You killed my wife."

Marjorie shrieked, her hands over her ears. "He did it—it was never my idea, it was him!" Roland still battled the ghost that had clawed her way out of the ground—Ritchie's wife.

Tim reached into his pocket and pulled out the pair of inscribed wedding rings. He tossed them to Ritchie. The rings disappeared when they met the phantasm's hand.

"Get out of here, Tim and Addie," Ritchie commanded.

"Go and don't look back." Ritchie offered a ghostly smile to Addie. "We will take care of the doctors."

Rochelle appeared on the ground at Marjorie's feet. The old woman screamed and fell over backward.

Tim eased the door shut behind them. "The ghosts are going to get their revenge," he said matter-of-factly. "Maybe that's what they've been waiting for this whole time."

"*Maison de Folie*," Addie mused. "The House of Madness."

They walked the rest of the way home in silence.

CHAPTER THIRTEEN

Going Home

Lisette hadn't shown herself in quite a while. "When you can't see me, it's me resting. Like sleep, for ghosts," she had explained before. Apparently, it takes a lot of energy for a ghost to allow themselves to be seen.

"I'm going for a walk," Michaela announced to her absent audience. "We've been here for hours."

A coyote yipped in the distance, then the thick odor of skunk musk filled the heavy air. She slapped her hand over her nose and dashed out of the cemetery. She strode over to the base of Scenic Mountain. It looked somehow different this evening.

Content, she thought.

Michaela hugged her arms across her chest. Images of her parents appeared without warning in her mind. The ghost in the closet with Lisette still bothered Michaela. Lisette hadn't mentioned her again, but jealousy was an ugly feeling and Michaela didn't like feeling it. Especially not with Lisette. She turned around and trudged back to the cemetery.

Mom and Dad, please be okay.

Sure enough, a fleeting image floated around the tombstones.

"Lisette!" Michaela dashed toward her. "I'm glad you're back. Or awake. Or whatever."

Lisette didn't look up. Her body arched over the graves of her parents and everything about her exuded sadness. If young phantoms could cry, this is how they would look. "I am so sad, *mon ami*."

"Thank you for all your help and for taking care of me. And my parents." Michaela grasped the wrought iron bars. "I was afraid when you disappeared this time—afraid you'd gone on to Heaven."

"I will never go. I will be stuck here. Alone forever."

Michaela opened the tiny fence and let herself back in. She was careful not to step on any graves. "I'll be here for you. And maybe someday, you can even play with my own kids in the closet." Michaela chewed her lip. "I promise, I won't ever sell the house and I won't let Mom and Dad, either." She paused. *It's now or never.* "Anyway, you have the other little ghost to keep you company in my closet. The one I haven't seen."

Lisette sighed. Still, Michaela continued.

"Maybe she can play with us sometime."

Finally, Lisette looked at Michaela. Her black eyes were hollow and lifeless. Something in them—or *not* in them— made her jump. "She came with your family, Michaela. She has always been near you."

Michaela paused and tried to swallow the knot in her throat. *I've been haunted?*

"She's your sister."

Michaela didn't speak. She couldn't. She'd watched her mother's heart break that day and she'd tried to forget it a million times since. The jealous bubbles were all gone, but other emotions she couldn't quite name were all over the place. "Can I meet her?"

"Yes. She's here now."

Tears sprang to Michaela's eyes. Lisette's visage faded a bit, like a stubborn candle flame in a steady breeze. Beside her, another figure's outline was visible in the low light. A beautiful young girl, about three or so. She grinned and clapped her hands. Though she didn't make any sound, her mouth formed the word perfectly. "Sissy."

"It's her first time to know that you see her, too," Lisette explained. "She's been with all of you since the day she was born—and died."

Michaela was powerless to stop her tears. So many things she wanted to say, wanted to do, wanted to ask. Instead, they all jumbled up in her mind and refused to let any of the questions out. She swiped at her damp cheeks and sucked in a breath. "Lisette, ask her if I ... Was it my fault that ..."

Juliette's grin faded and her hands dropped to her sides. Not comprehending, she stared at Michaela.

Michaela chewed her lip until she tasted blood. The black words were finally on her tongue. She spat them out like a piece of raw meat. "Is it my fault you *died?*"

Lisette let out a rolling laugh. "The living are so funny. Everything is always someone's fault. Michaela, Juliette says she loves you. Some things just—well, some things just *are.*"

The whuff of a horse made Michaela jump. "What's that?"

Lisette's fading image stood and turned around. Her thick black braids reflected the moonlight just like she was a real live girl. *Almost.* "It sounds like—"

"Michaela?" Addie's voice broke her concentration. "Michaela, where are you?"

Michaela waved. "Mom! Over here!"

Juliette's head turned unnaturally to the side. Her lips moved again, but still made no sound. "Mama."

The sound and smell of horses filled the air. Happy, laughing chatter was all around, but Michaela could understand none of it. It was all in French.

Lisette's mouth spread into a wide grin. "*Mamah! Papa!*"

Addie came to a stop by Michaela's side and looped one arm over her daughter's shoulders. "It's over, baby. The doctors are taken care of and everything's going to be fine."

Michaela was glad her mother was there, even though she seemed to have come right in the middle of something important for Lisette. Michaela wasn't exactly sure what was happening, but since her mother was here, it saved her the chore of having to explain it all later.

There's no way I'd be able to explain all of this and sound sane. She thought for a moment. *After everything happened with the ghosts and the Darkland doctors, I don't think sane will ever have the same meaning in our house.*

A woman's voice trilled through the air, though Michaela saw nothing otherworldly except for Lisette and a flicker of Juliette. Chains clanked together as creaky wagon wheels ground to a halt. "Lisette!"

"Mom," Michaela whispered, "how did you know where to come find me?"

"A dog came to the door."

Michaela balked. "Really?"

Addie shrugged. "Well, I assume it was a dog. Something came and barked at the front door, over and over. I didn't see anything. So, I followed the barking."

Michaela smiled a slow smile. "Dog. It must have been Dog."

Lisette's voice interrupted her reverie. "Goodbye *mon ami. Mamah* says I have done my duty, what I was left here to do. You were right, there was a purpose to my being stuck in your closet." She giggled. "And mine was to save you and let you see Juliette. Now it's time for me to go."

Mom's fingers dug into Michaela's arm. "Let you see who?"

Playful barking and stomping horse hooves surrounded them. Lisette's image flickered as she climbed into the wagon and momentarily animated the French familial scene. Lisette's dad, Gerard, held the reins and the ghost horses appeared eager to be on their way. Her mother, Aimee, was an older version of Lisette. Smiling and beautiful as she helped her daughter into the wagon, she whispered into Lisette's ear. Lisette giggled.

"*Mamah* says Juliette has to come with us now, Michaela."

Macky looked up at her mother. Tears ran in rivulets down her cheeks and pain contorted her features into someone almost unrecognizable. "Say bye to her, Mom. You can see her, can't you?"

Michaela pointed to the clump of grass where Juliette had sat moments before. There was nothing there.

Crushing sobs tore from Addie's throat. "Is t-this some kind of c-cruel j-joke?"

A sharp bark made them jump in tandem. Dog's fluffy young body illuminated right before their eyes. A young girl's giggle followed.

I got to see Dog. Just like Lisette promised.

Addie froze. Her lower lip began to quiver.

Dog's image flickered a bit, but the body Dog curled around did not. Juliette smiled a wide, genuine smile and clapped her hands again as Dog's fluffy tail patted her lap.

"There she is, Mom. My baby sister."

"Mama," Juliette mouthed. A squeak of sound accompanied the word. Juliette tried again. "Mama. Sissy."

"She couldn't talk a minute ago," Michaela whispered.

Addie stepped toward her lost baby and dropped to her knees. "My baby girl. My precious little Juliette."

"I love you, Mama," she said, then squealed and giggled again.

Addie reached out toward the little phantom, but her hands found only cool air.

Aimee spoke in broken English. "She saw your sadness. Wanted to tell her, no to tell *you*, she love you. She fine and happy. Will see you again someday."

Juliette's gleaming eyes widened. "Papa!"

Tim leaned against the wrought iron fence. Tears flowed freely from his eyes, too.

"Say goodbye," Aimee instructed. "Let her go. Don't make her stay here, scared and alone. Let her go now."

Dog let out a yip. The fluffy German Shepherd pup was eager to go, too.

Addie drew a fist to her mouth and Tim joined her on the damp ground. Slow and sweet, Juliette reached out a hand to her parents. Addie and Tim and Juliette sat together in a bittersweet circle.

"I can feel her," Addie breathed. Finally, her face, which had been contorted into planes of agony, broke into a smile. "I love you baby girl. I love you so."

Juliette's eyes had grown hollow, like Lisette's. Still, they shifted to Michaela. "Candy."

Michaela's jaw went slack as she made the connection. "*You* were the one stealing my candy! And I thought it was Lisette."

Juliette giggled again and stood up. "Bye bye," she said, flapping her little hand. "Bye bye."

She ran to Lisette, who helped her into the wagon.

Gerard snapped the reins and the ghost horses began to move. Dog jumped up and dashed behind them, barking happy barks.

"*Au revoir*," Lisette and her family called. "*Au revoir!*"

"Wait," Michaela cried.

Gerard's deep voice boomed. "Whoa!"

Michaela's hands trembled. "Mom, do you have any candy? Anything at all?"

Addie shook her head sadly. "No sweetie, I'm sorry."

Tim stepped over to his daughter. "Here Mack. I picked these up at the house." He handed her a bag of candy corn. "I bought it for you the other day but forgot to tell you." Michaela dashed over to the flickering wagon. She knew that she didn't have much time. "Here," she tossed the candy corn to Lisette. Just as the sugar had, when the candy corn met her ghostly hand, the pieces disappeared. "These are full of sugar. For the trip to Heaven. Please share with my sister." She smiled at Juliette, who waved again.

Then, they were gone.

A strange sense of peace enveloped Tim, Addie, and Michaela as they stood in the darkness of the field. The tall prairie grasses around the tombstones swayed gently in the night breeze.

"It's over," Tim said.

"Thank God we got this house and could help them," Michaela said.

"Yes, thank God," Addie said. For the first time in months, the world seemed crisp and clear. "And I'm so glad it's over."

She glanced at Tim as though they shared a private joke. "All of it."

Michaela looked around. The coyote yipped in the distance again and she wondered if he smelled like a skunk. A night bird called, long and low. The moon hung just over Scenic Mountain, bright and silver. Michaela stared at the mountain, which no longer loomed but also seemed at peace. Michaela welcomed the smile that spread across her face until her cheeks ached. "Life really is so very beautiful."

CHAPTER FOURTEEN

Emergency Room

"How do you feel, Addie?" Tim's voice mingled with the night air on the walk back to the house. "You had a pretty rough night."

Michaela interjected before Addie could answer. "Remember the owl attack, Mom? I think you're supposed to get a tetanus shot. And probably rabies, too." She looked up at Tim. "You can get rabies from an owl, right Dad?"

Addie sighed. "Well, we're all awake. Might as well make a trip to the Emergency Room."

Addie leaned closer to Tim. "You *can't* get rabies from an owl really though. Can you?"

Tim shook his head. "No," he whispered. "Unless ..."

Michaela led the charge across the empty street. In the still of the night, several fire sirens blared to life. "Unless what?"

"Well, what if it ate something with rabies, and had the blood on its talons?"

Addie flicked him on the arm. "Really Tim? Now I see who Michaela gets her thought process from."

Just as they stepped onto their block, several fire trucks, with lights and sirens, blew past them. They stood and watched them go by screaming into the night.

"There's a lesson in that," Addie said. "No matter what's happening in your life, it could always be worse. Just think of those poor people who the firemen are going to rescue. Everything that happened tonight, at least we didn't get caught up in a fire."

They pulled into one of the few empty spaces in the Emergency Room parking lot. Tim clicked off the engine. "Honey are you really going to write their stories? The patients, I mean?"

Addie glanced in the floorboard where the precious box was tucked neatly between her feet. "Yes. Yes, I am. Maybe the police will let me take copies tomorrow when we turn this in."

Tim chuckled. "Maybe so."

Addie sat between Tim and Michaela and stared at the TV that droned on in a corner of the Emergency Room lobby. It was bolted up there in such a manner, that if one watched too long, a crick in the neck was an obvious side effect. Michaela dozed with her head in Addie's lap.

Please baby, have sweet dreams. Don't let this night scar you for the rest of your life.

A rerun of one of the many Chicago medical dramas flashed on the screen. Tim let go a sigh and crossed his arms. "You know, when I had to explain that my wife was attacked by an owl, the receptionist looked at me like I'd—"

Addie stared at him. "Like you'd what?"

Tim puffed out his cheeks. "Like I'd lost my sanity."

"Excuse me." A man's reserved voice barely registered in Addie's ears, which still hummed from all the banging and shrieking. "Ahem, excuse me. Miss?"

Addie turned around. "I'm sorry, are you talking to me?"

He nodded. The woman at his side had her arm in a sling. She nodded, too. "Did I hear that you're an owl attack victim?"

Tim turned around, grinning. "Why yes sir, actually she is. Autographs are a dollar, pictures with the victim are five."

The couple exchanged a look of relief and chuckled. "Oh, thank heavens. Our GHG, Egg—"

"I'm sorry," Addie interrupted. "But what is GHG?"

The khaki-clad couple stared at her as though she'd asked what color the sky *really* was. "Great Horned Girl," they said in unison.

"Oh. I see."

"Anyway," the man continued, "Egg got loose in the storm. We've been looking everywhere for her. I'm afraid my wife slipped and got a nasty shoulder sprain in the process. I'm hoping—we're hoping—it was her who, well, got you. Though our sweet Egg would never attack anyone."

Addie smirked. "Well, I'm afraid you're scrambling up the wrong Egg." She chuckled again. Exhaustion and stress had taken a toll on her sense of humor, or lack thereof. "This owl banged into my window during the storm, and I don't think she was altogether friendly."

The woman with the slinged arm leaned forward intently, her horn-rimmed glasses making her eyeballs look huge. "What happened? Exactly."

"Well, something hit the window and I went out to investigate. When I got outside, the owl was laying there in the grass. When it heard me—er, when *she* heard m—she clawed me up pretty good then flew over the house. She was just stunned and not really hurt."

The woman snapped her fingers. "It was her, Randall. It was our Egg. I just know it was."

"How can you be so sure?" Addie hoped she didn't sound rude, but curiosity took her tongue and ran with it.

The gentleman with the soft voice fielded my question like a champ. "Oh, because when Egg gets scared, she likes to sit on my wife's shoulder. Or her arm." They shared a warm glance. "Of course, Alice always has her owl armor on, so she doesn't get poked or scratched."

His wife stood up. "May we have your address? So we can try and catch her before she runs off with the first GHW that comes along?"

Addie raised her eyebrows.

The woman cupped her face in her hands. "Oh, silly me. Great Horned Womanizer. There are quite a few in these parts."

Addie shrugged and tried to mask her bemused expression. "Sure, and best of luck to you."

The young couple dashed through the sliding double doors as a red ribbon scrolled across the bottom of the screen.

"Breaking News," it boasted in creamy white letters.

A live reporter spoke directly into the camera in front of a raging fire.

"Turn it up," Michaela shouted. "Please."

"Maybe that's where our fire trucks were going," Tim mused.

Someone turned up the volume. "I'm Jolie Rivera reporting live from what appears to be an arson attack on the condemned Big Spring Sanatorium building." Jolie brushed a lock of hair from her glossy lips. "We don't yet know how the blaze started, but authorities are investigating."

On the screen, two people were being led out by police—in straitjackets.

"As you can see," Jolie continued, "two people were rescued from the inferno, however both had managed to restrain themselves in straitjackets. Police say there is no reason to suspect a third suspect's involvement at this time."

Jolie pressed the earpiece into her ear and looked off camera, then nodded. "This just in folks," she told everybody watching. "The two people pulled from the blaze are Doctors Roland and Marjorie Darkland, who worked at Big Spring Sanatorium prior to it being condemned. Rest assured, we will bring you updates to this intriguing story as they become available."

Michaela looked at Addie through wide, blue eyes. "Mom, did you and Dad have anything to do with that?"

Addie shook her head. "No baby, I can honestly say that seeing this on the news is the last thing I expected today."

"Mrs. Smithfield," the nurse called from the door. "The doctor will see you now."

```
Dear Adelaide Smithfield,
Hello from This-N-That Literary
Agency! I am pleased to offer you
representation for your creative
nonfiction manuscript, Crazies.
We here at This-N-That feel your
proposal was a fresh twist on an
always intriguing subject—the pa-
tients at an insane asylum. The
personal photographs of each pa-
tient prior to their incarceration
is a wonderful addition, as well.
You mentioned in your query letter
```

```
that the patients you have chosen
to feature in your manuscript are
part of an open investigation and
that you were already working on
contacting their families for con-
sent. Please keep us updated as to
your progress in that endeavor.
Regards,
Angelique Waters
Sr. Agent
```

Addie printed out the email from This-N-That and tacked it to her corkboard that hung above her computer in the writing nook. She clapped her hands stared at the letter she thought would never come. "Tim," she called. "Honey? Come here!"

She waited for a moment, but nobody came.

She stepped into the hallway. "Tim? Macky?"

The TV rattled on from the living room. As Addie stepped quietly down the hallway, an air of uneasiness settled around her.

I thought all the weirdness was over now.

Sure enough, the tops of Tim and Michaela's heads were visible over the top of the couch. She crept up behind them. Just as she leaned down to say *boo,* Tim tilted back his head.

"Adelaide," he bellowed in his booming voice.

"Ahh!" Addie shrieked.

"Sheesh!" Michaela cried. The popcorn she'd been holding in her lap fell on the floor in a salted, buttery heap. Michaela scooped a handful of popcorn off the ground just as Frenchie, the standard poodle they'd adopted at the pound the day before, rounded the corner to help her finish off the buttery treat.

Addie smoothed her hair back from her face. "Guys, why didn't you come see my—"

"Hush honey, look," Tim said, turning up the volume.

Addie stared at the screen as Jolie, the reporter who'd done as she promised and covered every ounce of the Darkland doctors' saga, was live from the Howard County Courthouse.

"It has been decided that Doctors Roland and Marjorie Darkland are *not* clinically competent to stand trial for the deaths of thirteen patients, and one patient's wife, at Big Spring Sanatorium, while under their care."

The snapshots from their files lined the top and bottom of the screen as Jolie spoke. Rochelle's picture was first, followed by Ritchie's. The black and white picture of Ritchie and his wife on their wedding day was set to the side of the screen.

"What?!" Addie cried. "How could that judge be so—"

"Shh, Mom, Jolie's still talking."

"Judge Reyes has informed us that the doctors Marjorie and Roland Darkland will be confined to the residential psychiatric facility, Crestview Home."

The scary one with all of the complaints. The one I read about before we even moved here!

"The judge received an outpouring of letters begging that this be the outcome. Most surprising of all is that the sudden letter writing campaign was spearheaded by the Darkland doctors' three children. They said, and I quote, 'turnabout's fair play.' Thank you for following this story. This is Jolie Rivera, reporting live from Channel 2. Goodnight and God Bless."

ABOUT THE AUTHOR

Sara Harris and her family have made their home in places all over the world, from the majestic Oklahoma plains to the eclectic mountains of Italy—collecting inspiration and rescue animals along the way.

Sara is a member of the Romance Writers of America, Critique Chair of RWA's Hearts Through History group, Western Fictioneers, West Houston Romance Writers, The Catholic Writer's Guild, and The Transylvanian Society of Dracula.

Sara, her romance novel-esque husband, and their children make their home in Katy, Texas. She has her BA in Medieval European History and is represented by Julie Gwinn of The Seymour Agency.

Find out more at www.SaraHarrisBooks.com

9 781948 679343